中国古典文学英译丛书

Selected Poems of the Three Caos:
Cao Cao, Cao Pi, and Cao Zhi

三曹诗选英译

〔美〕吴伏生 〔英〕格雷厄姆·哈蒂尔 编译

Wu Fusheng　Graham Hartill

商务印书馆
The Commercial Press
创于1897

2016年·北京

图书在版编目(CIP)数据

三曹诗选英译:汉英对照/(美)吴伏生,(英)哈蒂尔(Hartill, G.)编译.—北京:商务印书馆,2016
(中国古典文学英译丛书)
ISBN 978-7-100-12162-0

Ⅰ.①三… Ⅱ.①吴… ②哈… Ⅲ.①古典诗歌—诗集—中国—三国时代—汉、英 Ⅳ.①I222.736

中国版本图书馆 CIP 数据核字(2016)第 078972 号

所有权利保留。
未经许可,不得以任何方式使用。

中国古典文学英译丛书
三曹诗选英译
〔美〕吴伏生　〔英〕格雷厄姆·哈蒂尔　编译

商务印书馆出版
(北京王府井大街36号　邮政编码100710)
商务印书馆发行
北京冠中印刷厂印刷
ISBN 978-7-100-12162-0

2016年6月第1版　　开本 880×1230 1/32
2016年6月北京第1次印刷　印张 8 5/8
定价:38.00元

目录
CONTENTS

前言 Introduction ··· 1

卷一 曹操诗选
Part One　Selected Poems of Cao Cao

气出唱（三首）　A Song of Breathing (three poems) ············ 16
精列　Spirit Breaking ··· 28
度关山　Crossing Mountains and Passes ······················· 30
薤露行　Dew on the Leek ·· 34
短歌行　A Short Song ·· 36
蒿里行　The Land of the Dead ·································· 40
对酒　Facing the Wine ·· 42
秋胡行（二首）　A Qiu Hu Song (two poems) ················ 46
苦寒行　The Bitter Cold ·· 58
却东西门行　Song of the East and West Gates ················ 62
步出夏门行　Stepping out through the Xia Gate ·············· 64

卷二 曹丕诗选
Part Two　Selected Poems of Cao Pi

钓竿行　The Fishing Rod ··· 76
十五　Fifteen ·· 78

短歌行 A Short Song	80
燕歌行（二首） A Song From Yan (two poems)	84
秋胡行 A Qiu Hu Song	88
善哉行（二首） How Wonderful! (two poems)	90
丹霞蔽日行 Crimson Clouds Hide the Sun	96
艳歌何尝行 Whenever	98
大墙上蒿行 Wormwood on the Big Wall	102
芙蓉池作 Written by the Lotus Pond	110
于玄武陂作 Written by Xuanwu Pond	112
杂诗（二首） Poems (two poems)	114
清河作 Written by the Qing River	118
代刘勋出妻王氏作（二首） Written on Behalf of Née Wang, Liu Xun's Ousted Wife (two poems)	120
清河见挽船士新婚与妻别作 Written upon Seeing the Newly-wed Boat Hauler Bidding Farewell to His Wife by the Qing River	122
折杨柳行 Song: Breaking a Willow Branch	124
寡妇诗 A Widow	128
于谯作 Written at Qiao	130
至广陵于马上作 Written on Horseback Arriving at Guangling	132

卷三 曹植诗选
Part Three　Selected Poems of Cao Zhi

斗鸡 Cockfighting	138

送应氏（二首）	Two Valedictions for Mr. Ying	140
赠王粲	To Wang Can	144
弃妇篇	A Deserted Woman	146
赠徐幹	To Xu Gan	150
公讌	A Party	154
杂诗（飞观百余尺）	Poem (The Tower is More Than a Hundred Feet High)	156
赠丁仪	To Ding Yi	158
赠丁仪王粲	To Ding Yi and Wang Can	160
三良	The Three Martyrs	162
赠丁廙	To Ding Yi	164
侍太子坐	Sitting in Attendance with the Crown Prince	166
野田黄雀行	A Yellow Sparrow in the Wild Fields	168
杂诗（高台多悲风）	Poem (A Sorrowful Wind Crosses the High Pavilion)	170
盘石篇	The Great Rock	172
仙人篇	The Immortals	176
游仙	A Trip to Join the Immortals	180
升天行（二首）	A Trip to Heaven (two poems)	182
七步诗	The Seven-step Poem	184
应诏	At Imperial Command	186
赠白马王彪	To Cao Biao, the Prince of Baima	190
浮萍篇	On Duckweed	204
七哀	Seven Sorrows	208
种葛篇	On Planting the Kudzu Vine	210

喜雨 Delighted by Rain	214
杂诗（仆夫早严驾） Poem (My Driver Brings My Carriage Round at Dawn)	216
鰕䱇篇 The Fish and the Eel	218
吁嗟篇 Alas	220
美女篇 On a Beautiful Woman	224
杂诗（南国有佳人） Poem (Down South There Lives a Pretty Woman)	228
杂诗（转蓬离本根） Poem (The Tumbleweed Is Torn from Its Root)	230
五游 A Journey in the Fifth Direction	232
远游篇 A Journey to a Distant Land	236
泰山梁甫行 A Liang Fu Song at Mount Tai	238
白马篇 The White Horse	240
豫章行（二首） A Yu Zhang Song (two poems)	244
薤露行 Dew on the Leek	248
箜篌引 Song to Accompany the *Kong Hou*	250
名都篇 On the Renowned Cities	254
杂诗（西北有织妇） Poem (In the Northwest Lives a Woman Weaver)	258
门有万里客行 There Stands a Visitor at My Door	260
闺情 Feelings from a Boudoir	262
情诗 A Traveler's Song	264
失题 A Poem	266

前　言

三曹，又称"曹氏父子"，是指曹操（155-120）和他的儿子曹丕（187-226）、曹植（192-232）。曹操是三国时期的一代枭雄。他占据北方，与南方的吴、蜀三分天下，死后谥称魏武帝。曹丕在曹操死后继承父业，并且代汉称帝，建立魏国，谥称魏文帝。曹植少年时才华横溢，曹操一度曾有意立他为太子。后因曹植行为放纵，曹操只好放弃，最终传位给曹植之兄曹丕。曹丕对此始终耿耿于怀，在继位后对曹植横加迫害。他曾令曹植于七步内作诗一首，不成便将他处死。曹植从容地于七步内吟出了著名的《七步诗》，令曹丕愧色满颜。这些故事，两千年来经由各种文学和艺术表现，在中国已经是家喻户晓。

在中国文学史中，三曹的诗歌创作也是一个世代流传的佳话。早在南北朝时期，人们便开始把他们相提并论。刘勰（?-520）在《文心雕龙·时序》中说：

魏武以相王之尊，雅爱诗章；文帝以副君之重，妙善辞赋；陈思以公子之豪，下笔琳琅。

刘勰进而把建安时期文学，尤其是诗歌的繁荣归功于曹氏父子。由于他们对诗歌创作身体力行，加之本人"体貌英逸"，使得当时"俊才云蒸"，各路英杰纷纷望门投止，献功效力。钟嵘（约468-518）在《诗品·序》中也说由于"曹公父子笃好斯文"，使得"盖将百计"的文士云集于邺，形成了"彬彬之盛，大备于时"的局面，使两汉以来"吟咏靡闻"、"诗人之风顿已缺丧"的诗坛为之一振，重现新生。不仅如此，刘勰还就以曹氏父子为代表的建安文学之特点做了如下经典描述：

> 观其时文，雅好慷慨，良由世积乱离，风衰俗怨，并志深而笔长，故梗概而多气也。

用现代批评术语对刘勰、钟嵘的上述评论加以诠释和补充，便是建安诗歌扎根于当时的社会历史土壤，既具有现实主义的内容，也充满了强烈的抒情精神和主体意识，因而突破了"质木无文"（《诗品·序》）的两汉诗歌之沉寂与局限，恢复了《诗经》、《楚辞》中的"言志"传统，为后代中国诗歌的发展起到了承前启后的作用。两千年来历代对曹氏父子诗歌的评论基本上不出上述文字所勾勒的大致轮廓。

曹氏父子之间的间隔虽然不长，但从他们的诗歌中，我们可以看到中国诗歌演变的一个重要阶段，即由民间杂言体向文人五言诗的过渡。在《诗品》中，钟嵘分别把曹操、曹丕、曹植列在下、中、上三品。他虽然没有对如此排列做出明确的解释，但是他对三曹诗歌的评语却向我们透露了其中的玄机。在谈到曹操的诗时，他只说其"古直，甚有悲凉之句"，只讲内容，根本没有涉及诗歌的体式和语言风格，言外之意无非是曹操的诗在艺术上尚还粗糙，故列为下品。相比之下，曹丕的诗虽然"率皆鄙直如偶语"，但毕竟"美瞻可玩，始见其工"；也就是说，曹丕之所以高曹操一等，乃是因为他的诗已经具有"美"、"工"的特色。到了曹植，则是把曹操的质朴与曹丕的美工集于一身，达到了"骨气奇高，词彩华茂，情兼雅怨，体被文质"的境界，因此"卓尔不群"。钟嵘身处梁朝，正是"文贵形似"（《文心雕龙·物色》）的时代，因而他的评判难免有所谓形式主义之嫌，后代不少论者尤其对其将曹操列为下品颇感不平。但是，由曹操经曹丕至曹植，中国诗歌由古朴至雅丽的发展演变轨迹的确清晰可见。曹操诗歌现存二十余首，皆为乐府歌辞。曹丕诗歌现存约四十首，其中除了乐府歌辞之外，已经有不少像《芙蓉池作》、《清河作》等完全以个人经历为题材的作品。在曹植的现存八十余首诗中，用于描写个人经历，如欢宴、离别、赠答等的作品更是比比皆是。随着题材的个性化，诗歌的语言也随之被赋予了诗人的特色，逐渐脱离乐府歌辞，呈现出追求形式工整、修辞浏亮的倾向。例如曹操的《气出唱》、曹丕的《折杨柳行》以及曹植的《五游咏》都是乐府诗，它们所描写的也都是游仙这一汉乐府中的常见主题，但它们的表现形式和语言特征却非常不同。下面分别征引这三首诗的前几行，以做说明：

曹操《气出唱》

驾六龙，乘风而行，行四海外，路下之八邦。
历登高山，临溪谷，乘云而行，行四海外，东到泰山。
仙人玉女，下来遨游。

曹丕《折杨柳行》

西山一何高，高高殊无极。上有两仙僮，不饮亦不食。
与我一丸药，光耀有五色。服药四五日，身体生羽翼。

曹植《五游》

九州不足步，愿得凌云翔。逍遥八纮外，游目历遐荒。
披我丹霞衣，袭我素霓裳。华盖芬晻蔼，六龙仰天骧。

曹操的诗为杂言体，全用口语。曹丕的诗已经成为工整的五言体，但仍带有较强的口语特征。曹植的诗则除了采用五言体之外，语言风格要比其父兄都更加精炼与优雅，实为后代文人五言诗的先声。明于此，我们也许便不会对钟嵘以己度人，求全责备，因为从文体进化与演变的角度来看，他对三曹诗歌的排列毕竟是言之有据。

早在二十世纪五十年代，余冠英先生便编选了《三曹诗选》（北京：人民文学出版社，1956）。我们编译这本《三曹诗选英译》，便是以这一选本为底本，并做了适当增减。除此之外，我们还参考了安徽亳县《曹操集》译注小组的《曹操集译注》（北京：中华书局，1979），夏传才、唐绍忠的《曹丕集校注》（郑州：中州古籍出版社，1992），赵幼文的

《曹植集校注》（北京：人民文学出版社，1984），以及刘跃进、王莉编著的《三曹》（北京：中华书局，2010），殷义祥译注的《三曹诗选译》（南京：凤凰出版社，2011），张强、田金霞解评的《三曹诗集》（太原：三晋出版社，2011）。《三曹诗选英译》共收入曹操诗十四首，曹丕诗二十三首，曹植诗四十八首，比例也与上述几个选本大同小异，反映了三曹诗歌的基本风貌。

  在英语世界中，三曹诗歌的翻译只是散见于各种中国文学、诗歌的选集中，而且数量不多。我们的这个译本，可算是开拓之作。至于我们对诗歌翻译的理念与方法，已经在此前出版的《曹植诗歌英译》（北京：商务印书馆，2013）的前言中做过说明，兹不赘述。

  在此，我们要感谢商务印书馆的许晓娟编辑，是她的建议和努力促成了此书的问世。能够继《曹植诗歌英译》后继续为商务印书馆这样在中国乃至世界上都享有盛誉的出版社翻译中国古典诗歌，我们为此感到荣幸与欣慰，并期待将来有更多机会合作。

吴伏生　Graham Hartill
2014 年 2 月

Introduction

The "Three Caos" refer to Cao Cao (155-220) and his two sons Cao Pi (187-226) and Cao Zhi (192-232). Cao Cao was the ruler in northern China during the Three Kingdoms era when the country was divided into three states. After his death, his son Cao Pi established the Wei Dynasty. He gave his father the posthumous title Emperor Wu of the Wei, and after his own death he was named Emperor Wen of the Wei. Cao Zhi, even when still young, was a brilliantly gifted poet. At one time Cao Cao intended to name him, instead of his older brother Cao Pi, the Heir Apparent; he had to give up this plan due to Cao Zhi's undisciplined life style, eventually letting Cao Pi succeed him. Cao Pi never forgave Cao Zhi for this. When he came to the throne, he repeatedly persecuted his younger brother. Once he ordered Cao Zhi to write a poem in seven steps or else face execution. Cao Zhi dashed out his famous "Seven-step Poem," which made Cao Pi rather ashamed. These anecdotes, via various forms of representation throughout Chinese history, have become familiar tales to people in different walks of society.

The Three Caos are renowned poets. In the history of Chinese literature, their poetic activities have also become legendary. As early as the sixth century critics have begun to name them together. Liu Xie (?-520), in his *The Literary Mind and the Carving of Dragons*, remarks:

> Emperor Wu of the Wei, who was then a prince and prime minister, had a deep love for poetry; Emperor Wen, who was then the heir apparent, was himself versed in poetry; the Prince of Chensi (Cao Zhi), wielded a brush whose style was brilliant as the sonorous jade.[1]

Liu Xie further attributed the flourishing poetic production of the time to the Three Caos. Thanks to their passion and patronage, talented scholars came to join their cause like "gathering clouds." Another critic of the time, Zhong Rong (ca. 468-518), claims that the Three Caos, together with those poets under their patronage, revived lyric poetry, which had suffered neglect and decline during the previous Han Dynasty.

In the aforementioned work, Liu Xie also gives a classic characterization of the poetry of the time:

---

[1] Translated by Vincent Yu-chung Shih, in *The Literary Mind and the Carving of Dragons* (Hong Kong: The Chinese University of Hong Kong Press, 1983), p. 463, with slight modification.

An examination of their writings reveals that most of them are full of feeling. This is because they lived in a world marked by disorder and separation, and at a time when morals declined and the people were resentful. They felt all this deeply in their hearts, and this feeling was expressed in a moving style. For this reason their works are full of feeling and life.[1]

In our current critical terminology, we may thus rephrase Liu Xie's comment: the poetry of the time was deeply rooted in its socio-political context, giving it a solid realistic footing and significance; since it originated from the poets' heartfelt engagement, it is suffused with a profound subjectivity. As such, the poetry of the Three Caos not only revived the ancient lyric tradition established in the *Book of Poetry* and *the Chu Songs*, but also paved the way for future development of Chinese poetry. Throughout the past two millennia Chinese criticism of the Three Caos' poetry has seldom gone beyond the perimeters set here by these ancient critics.

Although the time span covering the Three Caos is quite brief, we can nevertheless witness in their poetry an important stage in the evolution of Chinese poetry, namely the move from irregular folk meter to polished literati pentasyllabic poetry. In

---

1 Translated by Vincent Yu-chung Shih, in *The Literary Mind and the Carving of Dragons* (Hong Kong: The Chinese University of Hong Kong Press, 1983), p. 463, with slight modification.

his *Ranking of Poetry*, Zhong Rong put Cao Cao, Cao Pi and Cao Zhi in the third, second, and first ranks respectively. He offered no explicit explanations for this ranking, but his commentaries on their poetry might shed some light on this. In speaking about Cao Cao's poetry, he merely characterizes it as being "ancient, straightforward, and full of melancholy and sorrow." He makes no mention of its artistic feature, which seems to account for his decision to put Cao Cao's poetry in the lowest grade. Cao Pi's poetry, on the other hand, has begun to show some "beauty" and "refinement"; thus, although it is still colloquial in style, it marks an improvement upon Cao Cao's, hence deserving to be in the second grade. When we come to Cao Zhi's poetry, we witness a combination of "outstanding spirit and brilliant diction." Zhong Rong's was a time when artistic refinement was highly valued, so his judgment might have been biased. We can, however, discern a trend toward stylistic refinement in the poetry of Cao Cao and his two sons. Cao Cao has about 20 extant poems, all are old style music bureau lyrics. Cao Pi has about 40 extant pieces, which, in addition to music bureau poems, also include a few written at personal and social occasions. As for Cao Zhi, among the 80 or so poems that still survive, those that deal with personal and social occasions have greatly increased in number. As poetry became more personal, it required a more individualized medium and style. As a result, Chinese poetry during this period began to move away from the simple, formulaic, and folksy music bureau convention to become more attuned to personal expression and artistic refinement. To demonstrate this we may take a look at the following excerpts from three poems on roaming immortals, which is a recurrent motif in music bureau poetry :

曹操《气出唱》　　"A Song of Breathing" by Cao Cao

驾六龙，	I drive six dragons
乘风而行，	and ride the wind
行四海外，	beyond the Four Seas,
路下之八邦。	descending to the Eight States.
历登高山，	I would climb tall mountains everywhere,
临溪谷，	and gaze at the streams in valleys.
乘云而行，	I journey on clouds
行四海外，	beyond the Four Seas
东到泰山。	eastward to Mount Tai,
仙人玉女，	where the immortals
下来遨游。	and the jade girls gather to roam.

曹丕《折杨柳行》　　"Song: Breaking a Willow Branch" by Cao Pi

西山一何高，	How high is the Western Mountain!
高高殊无极。	Rising, rising, without termination.
上有两仙僮，	At the summit live two immortal boys,

不饮亦不食。

与我一丸药，

光耀有五色。

服药四五日，

身体生羽翼。

they drink no water and eat no food.

They give me a pill,

which radiates five-coloured brilliance,

having taken which, in four to five days

our body grows feathered wings.

曹植《五游》

"A Journey in the Fifth Direction" by Cao Zhi

九州不足步，

愿得凌云翔。

逍遥八纮外，

游目历遐荒。

披我丹霞衣，

袭我素霓裳。

华盖芬晻蔼，

六龙仰天骧。

Even the length and breadth of earth cramps my stride,

so I wanted to journey, just like a cloud, to the highest heaven;

there I may roam at ease, beyond the edges of the earth

and cast my eyes across infinite wilderness.

Clad in celestial robes,

donned in rainbow clothing,

my chariot's painted canopy bright between dark clouds

as six dragons haul me heavenwards.

Cao Cao's piece is cast in irregular meter and colloquial language. Cao Pi's has adopted a neat pentasyllabic meter, but still has a strong colloquial flavor. Cao Zhi's piece is much more polished and refined both in form and style; it is a precursor of subsequent literati pentasyllabic poetry, which became a major poetic form in the Chinese poetic tradition. Viewed from this perspective, Zhong Rong's ranking of the Three Caos is not without ground, although his treatment of Cao Cao has caused strong dissent among later critics.

As early as 1956 the eminent scholar Yu Guanying had compiled *Selected Poems of the Three Caos* (Beijing: People's Literature Publishing House). Our translation is mostly based on his book, although we have also consulted other recently published selections, as well as annotated collections of the writings by the Three Caos.[1] Our selection includes 14 poems by Cao Cao, 23 poems by Cao Pi, and 48 poems by Cao Zhi. For an account of our theory and practice of poetry translation, interested readers may consult the introduction to *Selected Poems of Cao Zhi* (Beijing: The Commercial Press, 2013). So far English translations of the Three Caos' poetry have been found only in various anthologies, and they are few and between. Ours is the first selection in English that contains most of their representative works in one volume.

We would like to thank Ms. Xu Xiaojuan of the Commercial Press. She suggested this title to us and worked diligently to oversee its publication. We feel fortunate and honored that after

---

1 For these works, please refer to the Chinese version of this introduction.

our *Selected Poems of Cao Zhi* we were given another opportunity to translate classical Chinese poetry for her prestigious press. We look forward to more cooperation between us in the future.

> Wu Fusheng   Graham Hartill
> February 2014

卷一　曹操诗选

Part One　Selected Poems of Cao Cao

气出唱（三首）

其一

驾六龙，
乘风而行，
行四海外，
路下之八邦。
历登高山，
临溪谷，
乘云而行，
行四海外，
东到泰山。
仙人玉女，
下来遨游。
骖驾六龙，
饮玉浆。
河水尽，
不东流。
解愁腹，
饮玉浆，
奉持行。
东到蓬莱山，
上至天之门。

A Song of Breathing (three poems)

1

I drive six dragons
and ride the wind
beyond the Four Seas,
descending to the Eight States.
I climb tall mountains everywhere,
and gaze at the streams in valleys.
I journey on clouds
beyond the Four Seas
eastward to Mount Tai,
where the immortals
and the jade girls gather to roam.
I drive six dragons
and drink jade nectar.
The waters in the river will soon be dry,
and no longer flow to the east.
To cleanse my stomach of anxiety
I drink jade nectar;
clutching the flask, I travel
east to Mount Penglai
and up to Heaven's gate.

玉阙下,
引见得入,
赤松相对,
四面顾望,
视正熴煌。
开玉心正兴,
其气百道至。
传告无穷闭其口,
但当爱气寿万年。
东到海,
与天连。
神仙之道,
出窈入冥,
常当专之。
心恬澹,
无所愒欲。
闭门坐自守,
天与期气。
愿得神之人,
乘驾云车,
骖驾白鹿,
上到天之门,
来赐神之药。

Below the jade tower
I am permitted entrance;
Immortal Chi Song is there to face me.
I look to the four directions,
and behold great brilliance!
The stars are rising,
their vital breath arrives along a hundred paths.
The immortals teach me that to know the infinite,
    I must close my mouth,
and cherish my breath to live ten thousand years.
Eastward I travel towards the sea,
to be conjoined with heaven.
The ways of the immortals
are dark and mysterious;
we must always attend to them.
A quiet and simple heart
has no greedy desires.
Sit behind closed door and abide by yourself;
heaven will meet with your breath.
I wish to live with the immortals,
to ride the cloud carriage
and drive the white deer
all the way to heaven's gate,
there to be given the immortals' medicine.

受跪之，
敬神齐。
当如此，
道自来。

Kneeling down to receive it,

I pay my solemn respect to them.

Thus

the Way will come on its own.

其二

华阴山,
自以为大,
高百丈,
浮云为之盖。
仙人欲来,
出随风,
列之雨。
吹我洞箫,
鼓瑟琴,
何闾闾。
酒与歌戏,
今日相乐诚为乐。
玉女起,
起舞移数时,
鼓吹一何嘈嘈。

从西北来时,
仙道多驾烟,
乘云驾龙,
郁何蓩蓩。
遨游八极,
乃到昆仑之山,

2

Mount Huayin
majestic in origin,
thousands of feet in height,
with floating clouds for its canopy.
Look! The immortals arrive
emerging from wind,
pursued by rain.
We blow our panpipes
and strike our zithers
in harmony!
We drink to the songs and dances,
relishing each second of today's pleasure.
The jade girls rise
and dance for hours,
how sonorous the drums and pipes!

When the immortals arrive from northwest,
they ride together on mist,
on clouds, drive dragons,
how luxurious and magnificent!
They roam to the earth's Eight Poles,
attain the Kunlun Mountain,

西王母侧,
神仙金止玉亭。
来者为谁?
赤松王乔,
乃德旋之门。
乐共饮食到黄昏。
多驾合坐,
万岁长,
宜子孙。

by the side of the Queen Mother of the West.
The immortals rest their chariots of jade.
Who are these arrivals?
Godly Chi Song, Wang Qiao,
De, Xuan and Men, the heavenly stars.
We drink and eat till dusk,
many chariots alongside one another.
We wish each other ten thousand years of life,
and prosperous offspring.

其三

游君山，
甚为真。
碓硙砟硌，
尔自为神。
乃到王母台，
金阶玉为堂，
芝草生殿旁。
东西厢，
客满堂。
主人当行觞，
坐者长寿遽何央，
长乐甫始宜孙子，
常愿主人增年，
与天相守。

3

We travel to Mount Jun,
with truly sincere hearts.
Majestic, craggy,
you are your own god.
We come to the Jade Terrace of the Queen Mother,
with its gold stairs and jade halls;
magical mushrooms grow near the palace,
and in the east and the west wings
guests fill every corner.
Our host rises to offer her toast:
May you live to infinite longevity,
and happiness accompany your posterity!
We too wish our host to live forever,
and abide in heaven!

精列

厥初生,
造化之陶物,
莫不有终期,
莫不有终期。
圣贤不能免,
何为怀此忧?
愿螭龙之驾,
思想昆仑居,
思想昆仑居。
见期于迂怪,
志意在蓬莱,
志意在蓬莱。
周孔圣徂落,
会稽以坟丘,
会稽以坟丘。
陶陶谁能度?
君子以弗忧。
年之暮奈何,
时过时来微。

Spirit Breaking

When life is born,
and nature molds its creatures,
all must come to their end,
all must come to their end.
Sages and worthies all succumb,
so why should I embrace this worry?
I wish to drive the dragons,
to live on the godly Mount Kunlun,
to live on the godly Mount Kunlun.
But deceived by the weird creatures up there,
I turn my mind to Mount Penglai,
I turn my mind to Mount Penglai.
Duke Zhou and Sage Confucius both are dead,
Great Yu was buried at Kuaiji,
Great Yu was buried at Kuaiji.
Who can traverse time's long river?
The wise then is not worried.
even as he is getting old,
and time presses on without him.

度关山

天地间,
人为贵。
立君牧民,
为之轨则。
车辙马迹,
经纬四极。
黜陟幽明,
黎庶繁息,
於铄贤圣,
总统邦域。
封建五爵,
井田刑狱。
有燔丹书,
无普赦赎。
皋陶甫侯,
何有失职?
嗟哉后世,
改制易律。
劳民为君,
役赋其力。
舜漆食器,
畔者十国。

Crossing Mountains and Passes

Between heaven and earth
humanity is most precious.
A lord is chosen to govern the people,
he sets the codes and laws for them.
By cart and on horseback
he woofs and warps within the Four Poles,
to suppress dark and nurture light,
to make common folks thrive and live at ease.
O, beautiful were such sage rulers!
They presided over the entire land,
they assigned fiefdoms and the five ranks,
they set up the land system and the penal codes.
One may burn the red criminal records,
but never issue universal amnesty.
Gao and Fu, ancient ministers of justice,
never neglected their official duties.
Alas, people in later times
changed the systems and altered the laws;
they made the people labor for their rulers,
and forced them to serve with all their means.
Shun had his utensils brightly painted,
ten states revolted against his rule.

不及唐尧,
采橡不斫。
世叹伯夷,
欲以厉俗。
侈恶之大,
俭为共德。
许由推让,
岂有讼曲?
兼爱尚同,
疏者为戚。

He could not be compared to Yao,[1]
who used uncarved wood for his roof.
People have mourned for Boyi,[2]
and set him up as a good model.
Extravagance is the greatest evil,
frugality a virtue for all men.
Xu You declined the offer to rule;[3]
if all behaved so, who would ever be litigious?
With universal love and equality,
distant strangers will all become relatives.

---

1   舜、尧为传说中的领袖。 Shun and Yao are pre-historic legendary rulers.
2   伯夷为商末王子。其父死后，他为让位于其弟叔齐，弃国而逃。 Boyi, who lived by the end of the Shang Dynasty, gave up his right to inherit the throne in favor of his younger brother Shuqi.
3   许由为古代隐士。据说尧曾要让天下给他，遭其拒绝。 Xu You is an ancient hermit; it is said that he declined the offer of kingship from Yao.

薤露行

惟汉二十世,
所任诚不良。
沐猴而冠带,
知小而谋强。
犹豫不敢断,
因狩执君王。
白虹为贯日,
己亦先受殃。
贼臣持国柄,
杀主灭宇京。
荡覆帝基业,
宗庙以燔丧。
播越西迁移,
号泣而且行。
瞻彼洛城郭,
微子为哀伤。

Dew on the Leek

During the twenty-second reign of the Han Dynasty,
wicked people were given power;
they were monkeys, wearing belts and hats,
making great plans with their little minds.
They were hesitant, having no courage to act,
so the monarch was taken on an imperial outing.[1]
A white rainbow spread across the sun,[2]
they too soon met their own disaster.
A traitorous minister took the nation's power;[3]
he killed the monarch and laid waste the capital,
he ruined the imperial cause and its foundation,
he burned the ancestral temple down to the ground.
People were forced into exile in the west,
weeping, wailing as they moved along.
I gaze at the outer city of our capital Luoyang,
I grieve and lament, like Weizi, in times gone by.

---

1 此指汉末宦官篡权，代少帝为政，何进等应对踌躇，终酿大祸。This refers to the usurpation of power by the eunuchs at Cao Cao's time. Due to the hesitation of court officials ("monkeys with hats and belts"), the Han emperor was taken as a hostage by the eunuchs surrounding him.

2 白虹被认为是灾祸的征兆。The white rainbow is usually taken as omen for disaster.

3 即董卓。他毒死汉少帝，自立献帝，独揽国政。This line refers to Dong Zhuo, the military general who usurped the monarchy briefly; he also had the young Han emperor poisoned to death and set up another puppet emperor.

短歌行

对酒当歌,
人生几何。
譬如朝露,
去日苦多。
慨当以慷,
忧思难忘。
何以解忧?
唯有杜康。

青青子衿,
悠悠我心。
但为君故,
沉吟至今。

呦呦鹿鸣,
食野之苹。
我有嘉宾,
鼓瑟吹笙。

明明如月,
何时可掇?

A Short Song

Let us sing with wine in our hands!
How long is a human life?
It is like dew in the morning,
I am grieved so many days have fled.
My heart is moved and stirred,
sorrowful thoughts are hard to leave behind.
What can relieve me of this sorrow?
Here is only the famous Dukang wine.

Green are the collars on the scholars' necks,
long are the considerations of my heart.
It is only for your sake, gentlemen,
I have been thinking and chanting.

Mewing and mewing, the deer cry,
grazing on wild wormwood.
I am entertaining honored guests,
zithers and pipes are played.

Bright is the moon in the sky,
when can I ever embrace it?

忧从中来，
不可断绝。

越陌度阡，
枉用相存。
契阔谈䜩，
心念旧恩。

月明星稀，
乌鹊南飞。
绕树三匝，
何枝可依？

山不厌高，
海不厌深。
周公吐哺，
天下归心。

Sorrow is born inside the heart,
it can never be brought to an end.

You crossed many paths in the fields,
humbling yourself to pay me a visit.
Intimately, we chatted through the party,
and recalled our old love for each other.

The moon shines bright among the sparse stars,
and the magpies are flying to the south.
They circle and circle around a tree,
not sure on which branch to perch.

Mountains are not concerned about their height,
oceans do not fret themselves over their depth.
Duke Zhou repeatedly spat out his food at meal times,[1]
all under heaven gave to him their hearts.

---

1 据《史记·鲁周世家》，周公曾说："我一沐三握发，一饭三吐哺，起以待士，犹恐失天下之贤人。"此处曹操以周公自况，以表达其求贤创业的急迫心情。The Duke of Zhou is exemplary statesman in ancient time (Zhou Dynasty). It is said that "he often held his hair during bath, spat out his food at meal, always ready to receive scholars for fear that he would lose the virtuous people in the world." Cao Cao is comparing himself to the Duke of Zhou in that he too would eagerly search for worthy people to help him in his cause.

蒿里行

关东有义士,
兴兵讨群凶。
初期会盟津,
乃心在咸阳。
军合力不齐,
踌躇而雁行。
势利使人争,
嗣还自相戕。
淮南弟称号,
刻玺于北方。
铠甲生虮虱,
万姓以死亡。
白骨露于野,
千里无鸡鸣。
生民百遗一,
念之断人肠。

The Land of the Dead

East of Hangu Pass arose the righteous heroes,
they raised troops to attack the wicked.
At first they agreed to gather at Mengjin,
but their hearts went out to the capital, Xianyang.[1]
The troops gathered, but their strength was not unified,
in hesitation, they moved in geese formation.
Ambition causes struggle in people,
soon they began to slaughter each other.
The younger Yuan declared himself emperor south of the Huai,[2]
his brother carved the imperial seal in the north.
Fleas breed inside the soldier's armor,
common folks die in tens of thousands;
their bones laid bare in the wilderness,
within ten thousand *li* no rooster crows.
One in a hundred is all that survives for the common folk.
My heart is broken by the thought.

---

1 即当时兴兵的各路人马心怀异志，意在篡位。In other words, the generals who rose to attack those wicked people all had their eyes on the throne.
2 此处的"弟"指袁术，袁绍之弟；后者为曹操在北方的主要对手。The younger Yuan is Yuan Shu, the brother of Yuan Shao, who is Cao Cao's arch-enemy in the north.

对酒

对酒歌。
太平时,
吏不呼门。
王者贤且明,
宰相股肱皆忠良。
咸礼让,
民无所争讼。
三年耕有九年储,
仓谷满盈。
班白不负戴,
雨泽如此,
百谷用成。
却走马,
以粪其土田。
爵公侯伯子男,
咸爱其民。
以黜陟幽明。
子养有若父与兄。
犯礼法,
轻重随其刑。
路无拾遗之私。
囹圄空虚,

Facing the Wine

Let us sing with wine in our hands!
In a peaceful time,
no official knocks at your door;
the rulers are wise and virtuous,
the ministers all honest and loyal.
People all behave with courtesy,
and avoid dispute.
Three years' ploughing gives nine years' food,
the granaries are full.
Grey-haired heads don't bear any burden.
Rain falls in abundance,
and a hundred grains await the harvest.
Galloping horses are held from battle,
and put to use by farmers in their fields.
Whatever their rank, the aristocrats
all love their people;
they punish the dark and promote the light,
they treat their subjects like parents their children.
When someone violates the rituals or laws,
he is sentenced according to penal code.
Lost items are left on the road untouched,
the prisons are empty;

冬节不断。
人耄耋,
皆得以寿终。
恩泽广及草木昆虫。

no execution is carried out, not even in winter.[1]
People of eighty or ninety years
get to live out their allotted span,
and even plants and insects are graced with favor!

---

1 在古代，极刑一般都在冬季执行。Executions are usually carried out in winter, according to ancient practice.

秋胡行（二首）

其一

晨上散关山，
此道当何难！
晨上散关山，
此道当何难！
牛顿不起，
车堕谷间。
坐盘石之上，
弹五弦之琴。
作为清角韵，
意中迷烦。
歌以言志，
晨上散关山。

有何三老公，
卒来在我傍。
有何三老公，
卒来在我傍。
负揜被裘，
似非恒人。

A Qiu Hu Song (two poems)

1

I climb Mount Sanguan at dawn,
how hard the road!
I climb Mount Sanguan at dawn,
how hard the road!
Cows collapse and can't get up,
carts tumble into the valleys.
I sit on a great rock,
play a five-string zither,
a clear and forlorn tune.
My heart is lost, disturbed.
I sing to utter my will,
I climb Mount Sanguan at dawn.

There, three elderly men
appear suddenly at my side.
There, three elderly men
appear suddenly at my side.
They wear coats over leather jackets,
and look different from ordinary folks.

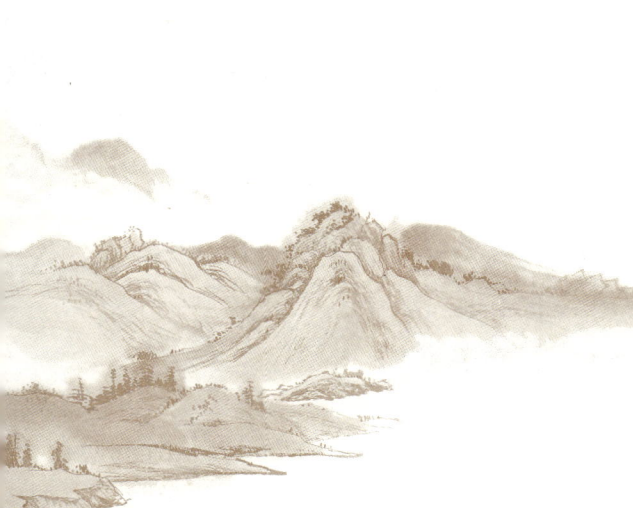

谓卿云何困苦以自怨,
徨徨所欲,
来到此间?
歌以言志,
有何三老公。

我居昆仑山,
所谓者真人。
我居昆仑山,
所谓者真人。
道深有可得,
名山历观,
遨游八极,
枕石漱流饮泉。
沉吟不决,
遂上升天。
歌以言志,
我居昆仑山。

去去不可追,
长恨相牵攀。
去去不可追,
长恨相牵攀。

They ask me: "Why are you bitter and full of self-blame?
What is it in your mind
that drives you to this place?"
I sing to utter my will.
There, three elderly men.

"We live on Mount Kunlun,
and people call us True Men.
We live on Mount Kunlun,
and people call us True Men.
The Way is deep but obtainable.
We visit all the famous mountains,
crisscross the Eight Poles,
pillowing our heads on rocks, rinsing our mouths with
    streams, and drinking from the fountains."
Deep in thought I hesitate,
then they rise to the heaven.
I sing to utter my will,
we live on Mount Kunlun.

They left, and none can catch them,
I always regret my being entangled here.
They left, and none can catch them,
I always regret my being entangled here.

夜夜安得寐，
惆怅以自怜。
正而不谲，
辞赋依因。
经传所过，
西来所传。
歌以言志，
去去不可追。

Night after night I cannot sleep,
melancholy, full of self-pity.
A straight and honest character
will find its match in song.
This old documents record,
as do my expedition to the west.[1]
I sing to utter my will,
they left, and none can catch them.

---

1 上面四行引述春秋五霸之一齐桓公的事迹。齐桓公凭借自己"正而不谲"之心，发现了向他献歌的宁戚这位得力助手；他也曾西伐大夏。曹操此处以齐桓公自况。The previous four lines allude to Duke Huan of the Qi, who was one of the five hegemons during the Spring and Autumn period. With his "straight and honest intention," he found singer Ning Qi, who later became a great aide to him; he also launched a western expedition against the Xia region. Cao Cao here compares himself to the Duke Huan of the Qi.

其二

愿登泰华山,
神人共远游。
愿登泰华山,
神人共远游。
经历昆仑山,
到蓬莱。
飘飖八极,
与神人俱。
思得神药,
万岁为期。
歌以言志,
愿登泰华山。

天地何长久,
人道居之短。
天地何长久,
人道居之短。
世言伯阳,
殊不知老。
赤松王乔,
亦云得道。

2

I wish to climb Mount Taihua,
and join the immortals in their roaming.
I wish to climb Mount Taihua,
and join the immortals in their roaming.
We travel past Mount Kunlun,
and reach the godly Penglai.
I hover between the Eight Poles,
accompanied by the immortals.
I hope to get magic medicine
and live ten thousand years!
I sing to utter my will,
I wish to climb Mount Taihua.

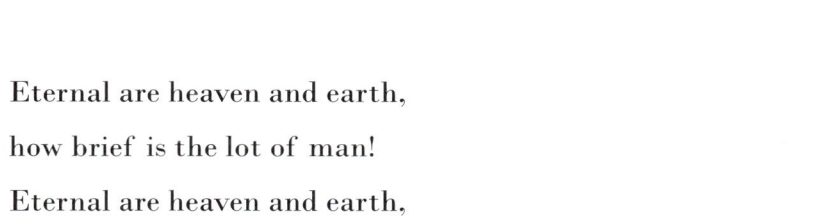

Eternal are heaven and earth,
how brief is the lot of man!
Eternal are heaven and earth,
how brief is the lot of man!
People say that Laozi
never knew old age;
Chi Song and Wang Qiao
are also said to have found the Way.

得之未闻,
庶以寿考。
歌以言志,
天地何长久。

明明日月光,
何所不光昭。
明明日月光,
何所不光昭。
二仪合圣化,
贵者独人不?
万国率土,
莫非王臣。
仁义为名,
礼乐为荣。
歌以言志,
明明日月光。

四时更逝去,
昼夜以成岁。
四时更逝去,
昼夜以成岁。
大人先天,
而天弗违。

I've never heard that we could do so,
I just want to live through my own old age.
I sing to utter my will,
eternal are heaven and earth.

Bright is the light from the sun and moon,
where is a place it does not shine upon?
Bright is the light from the sun and moon,
where is a place it does not shine upon?
The sun and moon bring forth the myriad things,
isn't the human paramount?
Ten thousand states and territories,
none but is subject to kingly rule.
Abide by benevolence and righteousness,
take honor in music and rites.
I sing to utter my will,
bright is the light from the sun and moon.

The four seasons pass in their turns,
days and nights become years.
The four seasons pass in their turns,
days and nights become years.
A great man may be ahead of heaven
but never disobeys its laws.

不戚年往,
忧世不治。
存亡有命,
虑为之蚩。
歌以言志,
四时更逝去。

戚戚欲何念,
欢笑意所之。
戚戚欲何念,
欢笑意所之。
壮盛智慧,
殊不再来。
爱时进趣,
将以惠谁?
泛泛放逸,
亦同何为。
歌以言志,
戚戚欲何念。

He does not fret about the years past,
but is worried that the world is not at peace.
Life and death all lie with fate,
vexing after it is foolishness.
I sing to utter my will,
the four seasons pass in their turns.

What is the point of melancholy?
let's make ourselves merry.
What is the point of melancholy?
let's make ourselves merry.
Our prime years and wisdom
surely will not come again.
We cherish every minute, always achieving more,
who will benefit from our efforts?
But letting loose ourselves and roaming at our ease,
what kind of conduct would that be?
I sing to utter my will,
what is the point of melancholy?

苦寒行

北上太行山,
艰哉何巍巍!
羊肠坂诘屈,
车轮为之摧。
树木何萧瑟,
北风声正悲。
熊罴对我蹲,
虎豹夹路啼。
溪谷少人民,
雪落何霏霏!
延颈长叹息,
远行多所怀。
我心何怫郁,
思欲一东归。
水深桥梁绝,
中路正徘徊。
迷惑失故路,
薄暮无宿栖。
行行日已远,
人马同时饥。
担囊行取薪,
斧冰持作糜。

The Bitter Cold

I climb the Taihang Mountain in the north,
how difficult, yet how majestic it is!
Its slopes are twisting like sheep intestines,
causing cart wheels to break.
Its trees are soughing,
the north wind making melancholy sounds.
Bears are squatting before me,
tigers are snarling along the road.
Only few people are found in its valleys,
hard falls the snow.
Stretching my neck, I give a long sigh,
my mind is full throughout the long journey.
My heart is deeply depressed,
I long to return to my home in the east.
The rivers are deep, the bridges broken,
I pace back and forth on the road.
Confused, I lost track of the old way,
when dusk comes we have no place to rest.
We walk and walk, leaving the day behind,
the people and horses alike get hungry.
Bags in hand we go to gather firewood,
and axe the ice to make our porridge.

悲彼东山诗,
悠悠令我哀。

I am thinking of that "East Hill" poem,[1]
reclining long in sorrow.

---

[1] 《东山》为《诗经》中的一首诗，描写征夫还乡。"East Hill" is a poem in the *Shijing* or *The Book of Poetry*; it describes the homeward journey of soldiers on the road.

却东西门行

鸿雁出塞北,
乃在无人乡。
举翅万余里,
行止自成行。
冬节食南稻,
春日复北翔。
田中有转蓬,
随风远飘扬。
长与故根绝,
万岁不相当。
奈何此征夫,
安得去四方?
戎马不解鞍,
铠甲不离傍。
冉冉老将至,
何时返故乡?
神龙藏深泉,
猛虎步高冈。
狐死归首丘,
故乡安可忘?

Song of the East and West Gates

Geese fly down from the northern steppes,
that indeed is a no-man's Land.
Lifting their wings they fly ten thousand *li*,
traveling and resting they form their patterns.
In winter they eat southern rice,
when spring comes they glide back to the north.
Tumbleweeds lie in the heart of the fields,
they float on the wind to distant places,
forever torn away from their roots,
never to meet them again in ten thousand years.
Alas, we soldiers on the road,
how can we quit heading out in every direction?
Our battle horses never shed their saddles,
our armor is never laid far from our sides.
Little by little, old age will creep upon us,
when can we go back to our homelands?
The divine dragon hides away in the deep valley,
the ferocious tiger steps out to the hills.
Foxes face to their mounds when they die,
how can I ever forget my homeland?

步出夏门行

艳

云行雨步,
超越九江之皋。
临观异同,
心意怀游豫,
不知当复何从。
经过至我碣石,
心惆怅我东海。

Stepping out through the Xia Gate

Prelude

The rain and cloud travel,
over the high banks by the Nine Rivers region.
Having heard different opinions from my staff,
I am hesitant,
not sure which way to take.
Now we have just passed the Jieshi Mountain,
and with a melancholy heart I come to the East Sea.

其一

东临碣石,
以观沧海。
水何澹澹,
山岛竦峙。
树木丛生,
百草丰茂。
秋风萧瑟,
洪波涌起。
日月之行,
若出其中;
星汉灿烂,
若出其里。
幸甚至哉,
歌以咏志。

1

Eastward I face the Jieshi Mountain,
looking out over the vast green sea.
How undulant are its waters,
its hills and islets standing tall.
Trees spring in copses,
hundreds of grasses, lush and strong.
The autumn wind is sighing,
making vast waves rise;
the sun and the moon move
as if arising from their midst;
brilliantly gleams the Star River
as if spreading out from their heart.
Ah, how lucky are we,
singing and chanting at our will.

其二

孟冬十月,
北风徘徊。
天气肃清,
繁霜霏霏。
鹍鸡晨鸣,
鸿雁南飞。
鸷鸟潜藏,
熊罴窟栖。
钱镈停置,
农收积场。
逆旅整设,
以通贾商。
幸甚至哉,
歌以咏志。

2

In the tenth month it is early winter;
the north wind hovers,
the sky is desolate and clear,
and dense frost spreads to every corner.
Pheasants cry in the early morning,
geese fly to the south.
Hawks and eagles hide themselves,
bears and tigers stay in their caves.
The shovels and ploughs are put aside,
the harvest lingering in piles.
Hostelries are now made ready
to entertain those who work in trade.
Ah, how lucky are we,
singing and chanting at our will.

其三

乡土不同，
河朔隆寒。
流澌浮漂，
舟船行难。
锥不入地，
蘴藾深奥。
水竭不流，
冰坚可蹈。
士隐者贫，
勇侠轻非。
心常叹怨，
戚戚多悲。
幸甚至哉，
歌以咏志。

3

Each place has its soil and ways of life,
north of the River is bitterly cold.
Flowing ice is all about,
making it hard for the boats.
Adzes cannot claw into the ground,
turnips and southernwood are buried deep.
The river water grinds to a halt,
men walk on the steady ice.
Scholars worry about their poverty,
vigilantes are unconcerned with unlawful acts.
I often sigh and lament,
and my heart is full of grief.
Ah, how lucky are we,
singing and chanting at our will.

其四

神龟虽寿,
犹有竟时。
腾蛇乘雾,
终为土灰。
老骥伏枥,
志在千里。
烈士暮年,
壮心不已。
盈缩之期,
不但在天。
养怡之福,
可得永年。
幸甚至哉,
歌以咏志。

4

Although the godly turtles are long-lived,
even they must meet their end.
Dragons may ride the mist,
but eventually they turn to dust.
An old steed may lie in the stable,
but his mind is set to ride a thousand *li*!
A hero may be ripe in years,
yet his valiant heart is still strong.
Human life is long or short,
it is not always nature's call.
With the help of self-nourishment
one can expect to enjoy longevity.
Ah, how lucky we are,
singing and chanting at our will.

卷二　曹丕诗选

Part Two　Selected Poems of Cao Pi

钓竿行

东越河济水,
遥望大海涯。
钓竿何珊珊,
鱼尾何簁簁。
行路之好者,
芳饵欲何为?

The Fishing Rod

Travelling eastward I crossed the Yellow and the Ji rivers,
and gazed at the shores of the great sea.
My fishing rod started to shiver,
and the fish's tail thrashed about!
Passers-by liked what they saw,
not sure what to do with their scented bait.

十五

登山而远望,
溪谷多所有。
梗楠千余尺,
众草之盛茂。
华叶耀人目,
五色难可纪。
雉雏山鸡鸣,
虎啸谷风起。
号羆当我道,
狂顾动牙齿。

Fifteen

I climb the mountain to gaze at the distance,
lush are its valleys and streams.
The Pian and Nan trees there are thousand feet tall,
the grasses and bushes exuberant.
Shiny leaves dazzle our eyes,
their many colors are hard to distinguish.
Pheasants are chirruping to each other,
tigers roar as winds gather in the valley.
Now my road is blocked by howling bears,
watching me fiercely, grinding their teeth.

短歌行

仰瞻帷幕,
俯察几筵。
其物如故,
其人不存。
神灵倏忽,
弃我遐迁。
靡瞻靡恃,
泣涕连连。

呦呦游鹿,
草草鸣麑。
翩翩飞鸟,
挟子巢枝。
我独孤茕,
怀此百离。
忧心孔疚,
莫我能知。

人亦有言,
忧令人老。
嗟我白发,
生一何早!

A Short Song

I lift my head to gaze at the curtains,
I look down at the tables and mats.
Everything looks like the old times,
but that man has disappeared.
Without warning, his spirit, his soul
abandoned me for its long journey.
Now I have none to look up to and to lean on,
my tears fall without end.

Mewing, mewing—the wandering deer cry,
and their agitated fawns cry back.
Birds flutter and flutter their wings
carrying their young ones to their nests.
I alone endure this loneliness,
and embrace my countless pains.
My heart is full of grief,
such as no one can understand.

The people have a saying:
sadness can make one old.
Alas, look at my white hairs,
how early they have arrived!

长吟永叹,
怀我圣考。
曰仁者寿,
胡不是保?

I sigh long, and lament,
longing for my dead father.
The virtuous are said to live a long life,
why was it not so with him?

燕歌行（二首）

其一

秋风萧瑟天气凉，
草木摇落露为霜。
群燕辞归鹄南翔，
念君客游多思肠。
慊慊思归恋故乡，
君何淹留寄他方？
贱妾茕茕守空房，
忧来思君不敢忘，
不觉泪下沾衣裳。
援琴鸣弦发清商，
短歌微吟不能长。
明月皎皎照我床，
星汉西流夜未央。
牵牛织女遥相望，
尔独何辜限河梁？

A Song From Yan (two poems)

1

The autumn wind soughs desolately, it is getting cold,
the trees shake off their leaves, dew turns to frost.
Swallows are returning, and swans flying south,
I think of you on the road, my Lord, my heart full of longing.
Regretfully you long to return, and miss your home,
why then, my Lord, do you linger in another land?
Your humble wife stays lonely in an empty room,
sorrow keeps returning, I dare not forget you,
as tears fall unheeded, dampening my clothes.
I pick up the zither, its strings emit a forlorn tune,
a brief song, chanted gently, but it can't last long.
The moon shines brilliantly on my bedcovers,
the Star River flows to the west, the night is not yet over.
The Herd Boy and the Weaver Girl meet each other's gaze,[1]
why then is there no bridge to bring them together?

---

1 传说中牛郎织女被天河所隔，各居一方，每年只有七月七日能够通过喜鹊搭成的桥梁相会。This refers to a folk legend: the Herd Boy and the Weaver Girl are separated by the Star River and are only allowed to meet each year on the seventh day in the seventh month, over a bridge formed by magpies.

其二

别日何易会日难,
山川悠远路漫漫。
郁陶思君未敢言,
寄声浮云往不还。
涕零雨面毁容颜,
谁能怀忧独不叹?
展诗清歌聊自宽,
乐往哀来摧肺肝。
耿耿伏枕不能眠,
披衣出户步东西,
仰看星月观云间。
飞鸽晨鸣声可怜,
留连顾怀不能存。

2

Parting is indeed easy, but reunion much harder,
mountains and rivers are distant, and the road far.
My heart is taut with missing you, yet I dare not speak,
I entrust my voice to the moving clouds, once gone,
    never to return.
Tears fall like falling rain, ruining my appearance,
who can avoid sighing when bearing sorrow?
I take out a poem and sing solo, just to comfort myself,
but joy flees while sadness rises, tearing at my soul.
Disturbed and leaning on the pillow, I cannot sleep,
I put on clothes to pace east and west through the gate.
Looking up to the stars and the moon I observe the clouds,
where a flying goose is singing a lovely song of the dawn,
I pay notice to it as I linger, longing and lonely in heart.

秋胡行

朝与佳人期,
日夕殊不来。
嘉肴不尝,
旨酒停杯。
寄言飞鸟,
告余不能。
俯折兰英,
仰结桂枝。
佳人不在,
结之何为?

从尔何所之?
乃在大海隅。
灵若道言,
贻尔明珠。
企予望之,
步立踟蹰。
佳人不来,
何得斯须?

A Qiu Hu Song

I was to meet with my beloved in the morning,
it is past dusk and she still hasn't come.
I have not tasted this delicious food,
and stopped drinking the fine wine.
I entrust my word to the bird in flight,
"Tell her I can no longer endure."
I stoop to break a violet blossom,
and stretching up I pick a cassia branch.
My beloved is not here,
so what do I gather them for?

Where would I follow you to?
To the corner of the mighty sea.
I'll ask the Sea God to meet you,
and give you a bright pearl.
On tip-toe I gaze out after you,
stepping and standing in hesitance.
My beloved has not come,
what am I to do this moment?

善哉行（二首）

其一

上山采薇，
薄暮苦饥。
溪谷多风，
霜露沾衣。
野雉群雊，
猿猴相追。
还望故乡，
郁何垒垒！
高山有崖，
林木有枝。
忧来无方，
人莫之知。

人生如寄，
多忧何为？
今我不乐，
岁月其驰。
汤汤川流，
中有行舟。

How Wonderful! (two poems)

1

I climb the hill to pick ferns
at dusk, finding myself hungry.
Winds rise from the streams and valleys,
frosty dew clings to my clothes.
Wild pheasants chirrup together,
monkeys chase one another.
I gaze back towards my hometown,
lush and dense the trees!
High mountains have their cliffs,
and trees their branches.
Sorrows arise from nowhere,
no one knows their origins.

Human life is just a sojourn,
why keep a sorrowful heart?
If I fail to take pleasure,
the years and months will march on.
Rapidly the river's torrents flow,
look, there is a traveling boat!

随波转薄,
有似客游。
策我良马,
被我轻裘。
载驰载驱,
聊以忘忧。

It drifts and moors with the current,
just like a traveler on his road.
Whipping my steed,
and donning my fur coat,
I march and I gallop
so to forget my sorrow.

其二

有美一人,
婉如清扬。
妍姿巧笑,
和媚心肠。
知音识曲,
善为乐方。
哀弦微妙,
清气含芳。
流郑激楚,
度宫中商。
感心动耳,
绮丽难忘。

离鸟夕宿,
在彼中洲。
延颈鼓翼,
悲鸣相求。
眷然顾之,
使我心愁。
嗟尔昔人,
何以忘忧?

2

There is a beautiful woman
with delicate brows, bright eyes,
and pretty ways, a tender smile
and a heart that is charming and kind.
She is versed in tunes and music,
an expert at song and at melody.
Her zither sends out moving music,
her singing is filled with fragrance.
Songs from Zheng and Chu resound and stir,
falling in harmony with Gong and Shang.[1]
They move my heart and stir my ears,
their elegant notes remain in the mind.

A separated bird nestles down at dusk
over there in the river isle.
It stretches its neck and shakes its wings,
crying sadly to seek its mate.
I look back in thinking of her,
my heart is downcast.
Oh, you people back in the past,
how did you forget your sorrows?

---
1 宫、商为五音中的前两音。Gong and Shang are two notes in Chinese scale.

丹霞蔽日行

丹霞蔽日,
采虹垂天。
谷水潺潺,
木落翩翩。
孤禽失群,
悲鸣云间。
月盈则冲,
华不再繁。
古来有之,
嗟我何言。

Crimson Clouds Hide the Sun

Crimson clouds hide the sun,
a rainbow hangs from the sky.
Streams murmur through the valley,
leaves tremble down to earth.
A solitary bird is missing its flock,
crying sadly among the clouds.
The moon waxes and wanes in turn,
withered flowers will never blossom again.
So it is since ancient times,
what do I have to utter but a sigh?

艳歌何尝行

何尝快独无忧?
但当饮醇酒,
炙肥牛。
长兄为二千石,
中兄被貂裘,
小弟虽无官爵,
鞍马駃騄,
往来王侯长者游。
但当在王侯殿上,
快独樗蒲六博,
对坐弹棋。
男儿居世,
各当努力。
蹙迫日暮,
殊不久留。

少小相触抵,
寒苦常相随。
忿恚安足诤?
吾中道与卿共别离。
约身奉事君,
礼节不可亏。

Whenever

When have we ever been happy, without a care?
So let's just drink our fine sweet wine,
and grill our fat beef.
My oldest brother earns a two-thousand bushel salary,
my mid brother wears a marten coat,
the youngest, I have no official rank,
but gallop around on my horse
mingling with aristocrats and high officials.
I'll wander around the baronial mansions
and pass my time away
at the gaming tables.
A man resides in the world,
and must make the best of it.
Hard pressed, the sun goes down,
his time does not last long.

When we were young, you and I were at odds,
but together endured the cold and the suffering.
How could I reason against your anger?
In the middle of this road I parted with you.
You ought to serve the monarch with all your strength,
and never fall short in courtly rites.

上惭仓浪之天,
下顾黄口小儿。
奈何复老心皇皇,
独悲谁能知?

Above, feel no shame before the blue heaven,
on earth, please feed your infants' mouths.
Why does my heart's anxiety grow as I grow old?
Who can understand my lonely grief?

大墙上蒿行

阳春无不长成。
草木群类随大风起,
零落若何翩翩,
中心独立一何茕!
四时舍我驱驰,
今我隐约欲何为!
人生居天壤间,
忽如飞鸟栖枯枝。
我今隐约欲何为?

适君身体所服,
何不恣君口腹所尝?
冬被貂鼲温暖,
夏当服绮罗轻凉。
行力自苦,
我将欲何为?
不及君少壮之时,
乘坚车,
策肥马良。
上有仓浪之天,
今我难得久来视;
下有蠕蠕之地,

Wormwood on the Big Wall

In sunny springtime everything flourishes;
plants and trees arise with autumn wind,
scattering leaves that scurry as they fall.
How bare and solitary are their stems!
The four seasons gallop away without me,
why am I left with this reclusive life?
Man lives out his span between heaven and earth,
sudden like a bird perched on a withered bough.
What has led me to this reclusive life?

Put on what is fitting for your body,
and pamper yourself with the most delicious food.
In winter wear the warmest marten coat,
in summer dress in the lightest gauze.
To work hard torturing yourself,
what good will that do?
Better when you are young
to ride the steady chariot,
whipping the strong steed forward!
Above us there is a bright blue sky,
I won't get to stare at it long.
Below there is the wriggling earth,

今我难得久来履。
何不恣意遨游,
从君所喜?

带我宝剑,
今尔何为自低昂?
悲丽平壮观,
白如积雪,
利若秋霜。
骏犀标首,
玉琢中央。
帝王所服,
辟除凶殃。
御左右,
奈何致福祥。
吴之辟闾,
越之步光,
楚之龙泉,
韩有墨阳,
苗山之铤,
羊头之钢,
知名前代,
咸自谓丽且美,
曾不知君剑良绮难忘。

I won't get to walk it forever.
Why not give yourself to roaming free
and answer your heart's plea?

Answer me, my precious sword,
why are you waving up and down?
Ah how smooth and grand you are,
white as accumulated snow,
and sharp as autumn frost.
Your handle is topped with rhinoceros horn,
your center enriched with jade.
You are carried by kings and emperors
to exorcise misfortunes and disasters,
to command all men to the left and right,
and to bring about good fortune.
You are the *Pilü* of the Wu,
the *Buguang* of the Yue,
the *Longquan* of the Chu,
the *Moyang* of the Han.
You are fashioned from Miaoshan's metal,
and Yangtou's steel.
Those famous swords of the past,
are all called beautiful by people,
but only yours is exquisite and unforgettable.

冠青云之崔嵬,
纤罗为缨,
饰以翠翰,
既美且轻。
表容仪,
俯仰垂光荣。
宋之章甫,
齐之高冠,
亦自谓美,
盖何足观?

排金铺,
坐玉堂。
风尘不起,
天气清凉。
奏桓瑟,
舞赵倡。
女娥长歌,
声协宫商。
感心动耳,
荡气回肠。
酌桂酒,
鲙鲤鲂。
与佳人期为乐康。

My hat rises up through the uneven clouds,
whose ribbons are fine brocade
decorated with kingfisher feathers,
lovely and ethereal.
They show off facial manners,
head up, head down, they radiate glory.
The *Zhang fu* of the Song,
the *Gaoguan* of the Qi,
these hats also said to be beautiful,
but are unworthy of a glance!

Push the bronze knocker, open the door,
and sit down in the hall of jade.
No dust is stirred by wind,
the weather is cool and clear.
Play the Qi zither,
let the Zhao dancers dance,
the singing girls sing;
their music is melodious,
it moves the heart, arouses the ears,
stirs the breath, and twists the sinews.
Pour out the cassia wine,
mince the carp and bream.
Let's make joy with the pretty ones;

前奉玉卮,
为我行觞。

今日乐,
不可忘,
乐未央。
为乐常苦迟,
岁月逝,
忽若飞。
何为自苦,
使我心悲?

they present jade cups,
and urge us to drink.

Today's pleasure
cannot be forgotten,
and has not ended.
Often we find our delight too late;
years and months pass away
suddenly, as if in flight.
Why should we let ourselves suffer
this ache in our breast?

芙蓉池作

乘辇夜行游,
逍遥步西园。
双渠相溉灌,
嘉木绕通川。
卑枝拂羽盖,
修条摩苍天。
惊风扶轮毂,
飞鸟翔我前。
丹霞夹明月,
华星出云间。
上天垂光采,
五色一何鲜。
寿命非松乔,
谁能得神仙?
遨游快心意,
保己终百年。

Written by the Lotus Pond

We take our chariots to roam at night,
and saunter around the Western Garden.
The double canals flow into each other,
fine trees meander along the river.
Low boughs touch the feathered canopies,
long branches reach into the sky.
A sudden wind rattles our wheels and hubs,
birds hover in front of us.
Crimson clouds set off the bright moon,
brilliant stars emerge from the clouds.
Rainbow drapes hang down from heaven,
how refreshing their five colors!
Our life span is never like that of Song and Qiao,[1]
who can ever hope to become an immortal?
Let us wander to our heart's content,
so we all may live out our hundred years!

---

1 松乔，即赤松、王乔，传说中的仙人。Song and Qiao, also referred to as Chi Song and Wang Qiao, are alleged immortals.

于玄武陂作

兄弟共行游,
驱车出西城。
野田广开辟,
川渠互相经。
黍稷何郁郁,
流波激悲声。
菱芡覆绿水,
芙蓉发丹荣。
柳垂重荫绿,
向我池边生。
乘渚望长洲,
群鸟讙哗鸣。
萍藻泛滥浮,
澹澹随风倾。
忘忧共容与,
畅此千秋情。

Written by Xuanwu Pond

We brothers leave together for an outing,
driving our carts to the west of the town.
Out in the wilderness vast fields have been tilled,
rivers and canals cross into each other.
How sturdy and lush the crops!
flowing waves stir up a moving sound.
Water chestnuts cover the green waters,
crimson blossoms shoot from lotuses.
Hanging willows make dark green shadows,
stretching along the bank of the pond.
We land on an islet to gaze at the outstretched island,
surrounded by happy flocks of chirruping birds.
Duckweeds float and flow all round,
lightly drifting under a gentle wind.
Together we roam, leaving worries behind,
and relish this eternal feeling.

杂诗（二首）

其一

漫漫秋夜长，
烈烈北风凉。
展转不能寐，
披衣起彷徨。
彷徨忽已久，
白露沾我裳。
俯视清水波，
仰看明月光。
天汉回西流，
三五正纵横。
草虫鸣何悲，
孤雁独南翔。
郁郁多悲思，
绵绵思故乡。
愿飞安得翼，
欲济河无梁。
向风长叹息，
断绝我中肠。

Poems (two poems)

1

The autumn night is long, so long,
and the northern wind, so cold.
Tossing and turning I cannot sleep,
so I get up, put a robe on, and pace up and down.
Too long, I realize, too long, I've been pacing,
white dew has dampened my clothes.
Lowering my head I look at the clear waters,
raising it, I stare into the bright moonlight.
The Heavenly River turns its flow to the west,
numerous stars crisscross in the sky.
Insects chirrup mournfully in the grass,
a solitary goose flies lonely to the south.
My mournful thoughts are dense and thick,
my longing for home forever lingers.
I would fly, but where are my wings?
I wish to cross the river, but find no bridge.
Facing the wind, I sigh, and sigh,
my inner being is torn apart.

其二

西北有浮云,
亭亭如车盖。
惜哉时不遇,
适与飘风会。
吹我东南行,
南行至吴会。
吴会非我乡,
安得久留滞?
弃置勿复陈,
客子常畏人。

2

In the northwest there is a drifting cloud,
it stands tall, like canopy over a cart.
What a pity that it fails to meet its time,
and by chance runs into a gale!
It blows me southeast,
and southward to the Wu-Kuai region.
Wu and Kuai are not my home,
how can I remain there long?
Let's put aside such talk,
a traveler often has fear of people.

清河作

方舟戏长水,
澹澹自浮沉。
弦歌发中流,
悲响有余音。
音声入君怀,
凄怆伤人心。
心伤安所念?
但愿恩情深。
愿为晨风鸟,
双飞翔北林。

Written by the Qing River

Twin boats play on the long river,
rising and falling with rippling water.
A string melody rises as we reach the middle,
its moving tone lingers in our ears.
Such music penetrates your breast,
its tone breaks our hearts.
What thought causes our hearts to break?
We only wish our love to be deep.
We would rather be the Chenfeng birds
and fly in a pair to the Northern Woods.

代刘勋出妻王氏作(二首)

其一

翩翩床前帐,
张以蔽光辉。
昔将尔同去,
今将尔共归。
缄藏箧笥里,
当复何时披?

其二

谁言去妇薄?
去妇情更重。
千里不唾井,
况乃昔所奉。
远望未为遥,
踌躇不得共。

Written on Behalf of Née Wang, Liu Xun's Ousted Wife[1] (two poems)

1

The curtain is fluttering in front of the bed,
having been set up to block the bright light.
I took you with me when I came here,
now I take you with me as I return.
I will keep you inside a bamboo box,
when will you ever be set up again?

2

Who says a sent-back woman is callous?
A sent-back woman has deeper feelings.
Even sent far away, one still does not spit in her well,
let alone the one that I served in the past.
To gaze homeward from far away is not hard,
but I hesitate—I will no longer be with him.

---

1 王氏因无子被其夫刘勋所出。曹植《弃妇篇》写的是同一主题。
   Née Wang was sent back home by her husband Liu Xun for failing to produce a son. For another poem on this subject, see "A Deserted Woman" by Cao Zhi.

清河见挽船士新婚与妻别作

与君结新婚,
宿昔当别离。
凉风动秋草,
蟋蟀鸣相随。
冽冽寒蝉吟,
蝉吟抱枯枝。
枯枝时飞扬,
身体忽迁移。
不悲身迁移,
但惜岁月驰。
岁月无穷极,
会合安可知?
愿为双黄鹄,
比翼戏清池。

Written upon Seeing the Newly-wed Boat Hauler Bidding Farewell to His Wife by the Qing River

We only just married, my lord,
but soon we must separate.
The cold wind stirs the autumn grass,
crickets follow us with their chirping.
The cicadas' chanting clings
like chill to the withered boughs
that now and then are torn apart,
so suddenly our bodies change.
Not for this my heart laments,
but sad to see the months and years gallop off,
these years and months without end,
how can we know if we will ever meet again?
I wish we were a pair of swans,
touching our wings, sporting by the clear pond.

折杨柳行

西山一何高,
高高殊无极。
上有两仙僮,
不饮亦不食。
与我一丸药,
光耀有五色。
服药四五日,
身体生羽翼。
轻举乘浮云,
倏忽行万亿。
流览观四海,
茫茫非所识。
彭祖称七百,
悠悠安可原?
老聃适西戎,
于今竟不还。
王乔假虚辞,
赤松垂空言。
达人识真伪,
愚夫好妄传。

Song: Breaking a Willow Branch

How high is the Western Mountain!
Rising, rising, without termination.
At the summit live two immortal boys,
they drink no water and eat no food.
They give me a pill,
which radiates five-coloured brilliance,
having taken which, in four to five days
our body grows feathered wings,
and lightly rising, riding on the floating clouds,
at a glance we travel billions of *li*,
observe the Four Seas,
recognizing nothing in their vastness.
Pengzu is said to have lived for seven hundred years,
but where, after all this time, is the proof of this?
Laozi left for the western region,
he has never come back.
Wang Qiao's story was but a vain rumor,
and Chi Song only left us empty words.[1]
Wise men know what is true and false,
only fools indulge in street talk.

---

1 王乔（王子乔）、赤松（赤松子）为传说中的仙人。Wang Qiao (Wang Ziqiao) and Chi Song (Chi Songzi) are two alleged immortals.

追念往古事，
愤愤千万端。
百家多迂怪，
圣道我所观。

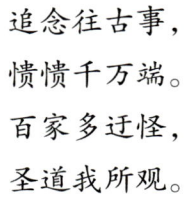

Take a close look at those ancient matters,
how confused and entangled they are,
a hundred schools of thought all teeming with absurdities!
I will follow only the way of our Sage.[1]

---

[1] 即孔子。 Confucius.

寡妇诗

友人阮元瑜早亡,
伤其妻孤寡,
为作此诗。

霜露纷兮交下,
木叶落兮凄凄。
候鸟叫兮云中,
归燕翩兮徘徊。
妾心感兮惆怅,
白日急兮西颓。
守长夜兮思君,
魂一夕兮九乖。
怅延伫兮仰视,
星月随兮天回。
徒引领兮入房,
窃自怜兮孤栖。
愿从君兮终没,
愁何可兮久怀。

A Widow

My friend Ruan Yuanyu died early.
I felt sorry for his lonely widow,
and hence wrote this poem on her behalf.

Frost and dew come ceaselessly down,
leaves fall from trees, how desolate!
Migrating birds cry out in the clouds,
returning swallows circle back and forth.
Sorrow moves the heart of your humble wife,
the white sun setting quickly in the west.
Each long night I long for you, my lord,
nine times each evening my soul strays.
I stand in sadness, looking upward,
the stars and moon follow each other.
In vain I crane my neck as I enter our house,
pitying myself for having to live alone.
I would rather follow you to death, my lord,
O how can I endure this everlasting grief?

于谯作

清夜延贵客,
明烛发高光。
丰膳漫星陈,
旨酒盈玉觞。
弦歌奏新曲,
游响拂丹梁。
余音赴迅节,
慷慨时激扬。
献酬纷交错,
雅舞何锵锵。
罗缨从风起,
长剑自低昂。
穆穆众君子,
和合同乐康。

Written at Qiao

I party with noble guests in a quiet night,
bright candles emit tall light,
delicacies spread like stars on display,
the jade cups full with the finest wines.
New tunes are heard from the strings,
their music roams, brushing the painted columns.
One tune lingers, followed quickly by the next,
we are deeply moved, our spirits rising to the sky.
We rise to toast to each other across the tables
while graceful dancers move in sonorous rhythm,
their silken tassels rising on the breeze,
and their long swords rising, falling, with their bodies.
Solemn and noble our honored guests,
together we take delight in harmony and health!

至广陵于马上作

观兵临江水,
水流何汤汤。
戈矛成山林,
玄甲耀日光。
猛将怀暴怒,
胆气正纵横。
谁云江水广,
一苇可以航。
不战屈敌虏,
戢兵称贤良。
古公宅岐邑,
实始翦殷商。
孟献营虎牢,
郑人惧稽颡。
充国务耕殖,
先零自破亡。

Written on Horseback Arriving at Guangling

I survey our troops by the Yangtze River,
how rapidly flow its torrential waters!
The soldiers' spears form a mountain forest,
their armor gleaming in the sunlight.
Our generals' hearts embrace great anger,
their courage fills up all directions of the earth.
Who says that the River is wide?
We can cross it on a raft of reeds.
Without a single fight we subdue our enemies,
we put away our weapons to gain a virtuous name.
The Grand Duke of Zhou went to live at Qi,
beginning the process of overthrowing the Shang.[1]
When Meng Xian was the magistrate of Hulao,
the people of Zheng kneed down in awe.
To make the country rich one must plant crops,
for when crops wither a nation will fall to ruin.

---

1 古公，即周太公，周朝的早期领袖。他曾为避免与戎狄冲突而迁居岐山之下，当时人民多追随他，最终灭商。The Grand Duke of Zhou was one of the early leaders of the Zhou Dynasty. He went to live at Mount Qi to avoid fighting with his enemies; many people followed him there, thus beginning the process of overthrowing the Shang Dynasty.

兴农淮泗间,
筑室都徐方。
量宜运权略,
六军咸悦康。
岂如东山诗,
悠悠多忧伤?

We cultivate farming between the Huai and the Si,
build homes and garrisons around the land of Xu.
When we make proper strategies and plans,
all six armies will be happy and robust.
Why must we chant the "East Hill" song,
sighing over endless grief?[1]

1　参照曹操《苦寒行》最后两句。See the last two lines of Cao Cao's "Bitter Cold."

卷三　曹植诗选

Part Three　Selected Poems of Cao Zhi

斗鸡

游目极妙伎,
清听厌宫商。
主人寂无为,
众宾进乐方。
长筵坐戏客,
斗鸡观闲房。
群雄正翕赫,
双翘自飞扬。
挥羽邀清风,
悍目发朱光。
觜落轻毛散,
严距往往伤。
长鸣入青云,
扇翼独翱翔。
愿蒙狸膏助,
常得擅此场。

Cockfighting

His lordship's eyes have seen the most beautiful dances,
his hearing is blunted with music.
He sits all day with nothing to do,
while guests do trick after trick to try to amuse him.
Guests take their places, on a long straw mat
in the spacious quiet room to watch the cockfight.
The choicest cocks parade their ferocity,
raising their tails up high, and
fanning their wings, stirring up a wind,
their truculent eyes emitting rays of scarlet light.
Their beaks fall, their feathers are ripped
from bodies bloodied by every heavy stroke of claw.
Then the victor's crow erupts into the sky,
he wafts his wings and prances, up and down.
Adorn his head with the grease from a dog raccoon,
that he may reign forever in the pit!

送应氏（二首）

其一

步登北邙阪，
遥望洛阳山。
洛阳何寂寞，
宫室尽烧焚。
垣墙皆顿擗，
荆棘上参天。
不见旧耆老，
但睹新少年。
侧足无行径，
荒畴不复田。
游子久不归，
不识陌与阡。
中野何萧条，
千里无人烟。
念我平生亲，
气结不能言。

Two Valedictions for Mr. Ying

1

I climbed the slope at Beimang
and gazed across at Mount Luoyang, far away.
Deathly and silent was Luoyang,
the palaces all burned down to the ground,
all their walls destroyed,
and thorn trees sprouting, high as heaven.
All my old acquaintances were gone
and only youngsters came and went from view.
My feet could find no path to tread,
what once were fields, deserts now,
and travelers, returning home at last,
could find no path to walk across the fields.
How desolate this wilderness,
thousands of *li*, not a soul, not a curl of kitchen smoke.
And I thought of my lifelong relations and friends,
choking, my throat deprived of speech.

其二

清时难屡得,
嘉会不可常。
天地无终极,
人命若朝霜。
愿得展嬿婉,
我友之朔方。
亲昵并集送,
置酒此河阳。
中馈岂独薄,
宾饮不尽觞。
爱至望苦深,
岂不愧中肠?
山川阻且远,
别促会日长。
愿为比翼鸟,
施翮起高翔。

2

Times of peace don't come that often,
the beauty of union doesn't last for long.
Heaven and earth have no limit in time,
the life of man is like the dew at dawn.
I'd like to say how my heart was moved,
when you, my friend, were leaving for the north.
Friends and relatives all gathered to see you off
and wine flowed freely, by the River's north bank.
The food and the drink were far from simple fare,
but none of the guests could empty their bowls.
Too deep in love, it's a bottomless sorrow,
how can my heart not be ripped with remorse?
The road is long, over mountains and valleys, unsteady,
the parting is brief, but the absence is long.
And I wish that we were the Biyi birds,[1]
spreading our wings and flying together,
                higher and higher.

---

1 一种不成对不飞的鸟，象征友谊与爱情。A kind of birds that only fly in pair, hence a symbol of friendship and love.

赠王粲

端坐苦愁思,
揽衣起西游。
树木发春华,
清池激长流。
中有孤鸳鸯,
哀鸣求匹俦。
我愿执此鸟,
惜哉无轻舟。
欲归忘故道,
顾望但怀愁。
悲风鸣我侧,
羲和逝不留。
重阴润万物,
何惧泽不周?
谁令君多念,
自使怀百忧。

To Wang Can

I sat bolt upright, distress possessed me.
Clutching my clothes I set out for the Western Garden.[1]
There the trees and flowers are blossoming
and streams are hurtling down to the clear pools.
I heard the cry of a solo mandarin duck,
chirping sadly, searching for its mate.
And I wanted to go to this bird,
but could find no boat on the water.
I longed to return, but forget the old path
and looking back, such sorrow fills my veins.
The wind in mourning moans at my side,
the sun proceeds, unwilling to take his rest.
The dense raincloud nourishes everything,
why should we fear its favor is limited?
Who is it that spurs this anxiety,
granting you this hundred years' worry?

---

1 "西游"当指游西园,即邺城之铜雀台。参见曹丕《芙蓉池作》。"Western Garden" refers to the "Bronze Bird Garden" in the town of Ye. See also Cao Po's "Written by the Lotus Pond."

弃妇篇

石榴植前庭,
绿叶摇缥青。
丹华灼烈烈,
璀采有光荣。
光荣晔流离,
可以处淑灵。
有鸟飞来集,
拊翼以悲鸣。
悲鸣夫何为?
丹华实不成。
拊心长叹息,
无子当归宁。
有子月经天,
无子若流星。
天月相终始,
流星没无精。
栖迟失所宜,
下与瓦石并。
忧怀从中来,
叹息通鸡鸣。

A Deserted Woman

A pomegranate tree grew in front of the courtyard,
wind blew on the leaves, flashing their green and white.
Its flowers were beaming, its flowers were shining,
mixed together brilliantly
like brilliantly colored glazes,
fitting spot for a phoenix to rest.
Birds came to gather, and one
patted its wings and cried mournfully.
What made it cry mournfully?
"I am a beautiful flower, but bear no fruit."
She patted her breast and sighed.
"A woman without a son must return to her mother's home.
A woman who has a son is like the moon, floating across
    the sky;
Without one, she is just a shooting star.
The sky and moon move together from start to finish,
the shooting star, at a glance, is gone out.
With no place to stay
it decays into stones and dust.
Sadness rises from my heart,
my sobbing and sighing go on till cockcrow.

反侧不能寐,
逍遥于前庭。
踟蹰还入房,
肃肃帷幕声。
搴帷更摄带,
抚弦调鸣筝。
慷慨有余音,
要妙悲且清。
收泪长叹息,
何以负神灵?
招摇待霜露,
何必春夏成?
晚获为良实,
愿君且安宁。

I toss and turn, unable to sleep,
I cross and recross the courtyard.
Haltingly, I go back to my chamber,
my bed curtains rustle the wind.
I tie them up with a sash
then pick up the zither
and play a tune so moving, lingering,
the very atmosphere fills with pure, mournful music.
I choke back tears, sigh once more,
what could I have done to cross the godly spirit?"
But cassias never show off till the days of fog and dew,
it doesn't have to be only summer or spring.
The fruit that is gathered late is the finest fruit.
Please be patient and rest assured.

赠徐幹

惊风飘白日,
忽然归西山。
圆景光未满,
众星粲以繁。
志士营世业,
小人亦不闲。
聊且夜行游,
游彼双阙间。
文昌郁云兴,
迎风高中天。
春鸠鸣飞栋,
流猋激棂轩。
顾念蓬室士,
贫贱诚足怜。
薇藿弗充虚,
皮褐犹不全。
慷慨有悲心,
兴文自成篇。
宝弃怨何人?
和氏有其愆。

To Xu Gan

The storm-wind blows the sunlight
suddenly back to the western hill.
The moon is not yet full,
the sky dense with stars.
Noble scholars work hard for the good of the world,
neither are those petty men idle.
Midnight let me travel, and
travel between palaces' twin towers:
Wenchang, cloud-penetrating, magnificent,
and Yingfeng, reaching up to the sky.
Turtledoves call between the flying beams,
a whirling wind knocks at the latticed windows.
I think of the scholar living in a hut,
I pity his pennilessness and humility;
wild herbs his diet, inadequate,
short coat his cover, incomplete.
With high emotions in his breast,
he writes at inspiration's bidding.
Whom should be faulted for the neglected ruby?
He who once possessed it was also to blame.

弹冠俟知己,
知己谁不然?
良田无晚岁,
膏泽多丰年。
亮怀玙璠美,
积久德愈宣。
亲交义在敦,
申章复何言?

You dust your cap[1] and await your bosom friends,
but which of your bosom friends is not also waiting?
It's never too late to cultivate a fertile field,
and good rich land has many a harvest year.
Cherish the pearl in your heart,
cultivated virtue grows even brighter.
We need friends to urge us ahead:
this, the poem, says it all.

---

1 "弹冠"表示准备出仕。A gesture indicating one is ready to serve in the government.

公讌

公子爱敬客,
终宴不知疲。
清夜游西园,
飞盖相追随。
明月澄清景,
列宿正参差。
秋兰被长坂,
朱华冒绿池。
潜鱼跃清波,
好鸟鸣高枝。
神飙接丹毂,
轻辇随风移。
飘飖放志意,
千秋长若斯。

A Party

The prince loves to play host
and as the banquet ends, he's lively as ever.
In midnight quiet we wander the Western Garden,
feathered canopy after feathered canopy
in the brilliant moonlight;
between the scattered stars the constellations cluster.
Autumn-scented violets cover the long slope,
red lotuses spreading over green ponds.
Fish patrol the depths, and there, one leaps!
Bright-plumed birds are singing in the highest boughs.
A lively wind rises, rattling the painted wheels,
the weightless chariots drift before it.
Carefree, we are light at heart; let us stay
forever, is my dream, like this.

杂诗

飞观百余尺,
临牖御棂轩。
远望周千里,
朝夕见平原。
烈士多悲心,
小人偷自闲。
国仇亮不塞,
甘心思丧元。
拊剑西南望,
思欲赴太山。
弦急悲声发,
聆我慷慨言。

Poem

The tower is more than a hundred feet high,
I stand by the window, leaning on the rail.
In every direction I see a thousand *li*,
mornings and evenings find me staring across the plains.
The hero often bears a melancholy heart,
the coward finds a lot of leisure in his life.
Our foes are still to be wiped out,
and for this I am prepared to give up my head.
I grasp my sword to gaze southwest,
longing to ascend Mount Tai.
The zither hastens and moans.
Oh hear, my heroic words!

赠丁仪

初秋凉气发,
庭树微销落。
凝霜依玉除,
清风飘飞阁。
朝云不归山,
霖雨成川泽。
黍稷委畴陇,
农夫安所获?
在贵多忘贱,
为恩谁能博?
狐白足御冬,
焉念无衣客?
思慕延陵子,
宝剑非所惜。
子其宁尔心,
亲交义不薄。

To Ding Yi

In early autumn, a chill comes into the air,
the leaves start to fall in the courtyard,
the jade staircase is carpeted with frost
and a wind blows in and out of the flying tower.
The morning cloud fails to return to the mountains,
it rains, and the rain forms pools and rivers.
Crops decay in the fields
and gather no gain to the farmers.
The rich too often forgets the poor and the humble,
where is he who shares his bounty with all?
Fox skin is enough to keep one warm in winter,
why think of those who have nothing to put on?
In admiration, my mind turns toward Prince Yanling[1]
who gave away his priceless sword with no regrets.
May your heart remain at rest;
our friendship isn't superficial.

---

1 延陵子，即吴季札，春秋时期一历史人物。Prince Yanling is a historical figure during the Spring and Autumn period.

赠丁仪王粲

从军度函谷,
驱马过西京。
山岑高无极,
泾渭扬浊清。
壮哉帝王居,
佳丽殊百城。
员阙出浮云,
承露概泰清。
皇佐扬天惠,
四海无交兵。
权家虽爱胜,
全国为令名。
君子在末位,
不能歌德声。
丁生怨在朝,
王子欢自营。
欢怨非贞则,
中和诚可经。

To Ding Yi and Wang Can

Riding out with the troops I passed Hangu,
our horses bore us on, by way of Chang'an.
In that region, the mountains were high beyond limit,
and in the Jing and Wei flow muddy and clear waters.
Splendid indeed are the imperial palaces,
surpassing in grandeur a hundred cities!
Their round columns pierce the floating clouds,
with plates holding dew from the Great Clearing.[1]
Our Imperial Aide[2] dispenses his heavenly favor,
all within the Four Seas lies free from battle.
The generals may love to win their victories
but serving the entire country makes for greater fame.
You, my friends, are not in high positions
and therefore cannot sing the praises of his virtue.
Ding Yi complains: he has to stay at court,
Wang Can devotes himself to his private things.
Both may not be the right behavior,
better to abide by your balanced heart!

---

1 "泰清"指天。"Great Clearing" refers to sky.
2 "皇佐"指曹操。"Imperial Aide" refers to Cao Cao, Cao Zhi's father.

三良

功名不可为,
忠义我所安。
秦穆先下世,
三臣皆自残。
生时等荣乐,
既没同忧患。
谁言捐躯易,
杀身诚独难。
揽涕登君墓,
临穴仰天叹。
长夜何冥冥,
一往不复还。
黄鸟为悲鸣,
哀哉伤肺肝。

The Three Martyrs[1]

Fame and success cannot be conjured by man,
loyalty is what we depend upon.
Duke Mu of Qin died first,
then the Three Martyrs, willing sacrifices.
While he lived they shared his glory and pleasure,
when he died, his fears and misery.
Who dares say that to die is a simple thing?
It is surely the greatest trial of all.
Holding back tears, they walked to his grave,
lifting their faces to the sky, they sighed.
Dark is the night, without end;
when they were gone, there was no return.
The yellow bird is mourning for them,
and grief is an ache in my breast.

---

1 "三良"指为秦穆公殉葬的奄息、仲行、鍼虎。"Three Martyrs" refer to Yanxi, Zhonghang, and Qianshu; when their patron, Duke Mu of Qin (fl. seventh century BC) died, they followed him to his grave as human sacrifices.

赠丁廙

嘉宾填城阙,
丰膳出中厨。
吾与二三子,
曲宴此城隅。
秦筝发西气,
齐瑟扬东讴。
肴来不虚归,
觞至反无余。
我岂狎异人?
朋友与我俱。
大国多良材,
譬海出明珠。
君子义休偫,
小人德无储。
积善有余庆,
荣枯立可须。
滔荡固大节,
世俗多所拘。
君子通大道,
无愿为世儒。

To Ding Yi

The town's gatehouse was brimming with noble guests,
delicacies in plenty issued from the kitchen.
I and several very good friends
were holding a private party in a corner of the town.
Music in western style was played on the zither of Qin,
eastern melodies sang from the harp of Qi.
All the bowls went back to the kitchen clean,
the wine cups drained of every drop.
I am not one to endear myself to strangers,
I only have my closest companions about me.
A great state teems with the greatest talents,
just as the sea breeds precious pearls.
A gentleman's virtue is beautifully abundant,
the petty man's is stunted in growth.
Storing virtue will bring happiness and fortune,
rise and fall must be anticipated every moment.
Magnanimity is surely a noble conduct,
yet the world's custom often restricts us.
A gentleman must penetrate the very truth of life,
untrammeled by the world's pedants.

侍太子坐

白日曜青春，
时雨静飞尘。
寒冰辟炎景，
凉风飘我身。
清醴盈金觞，
肴馔纵横陈。
齐人进奇乐，
歌者出西秦。
翩翩我公子，
机巧忽若神。

Sitting in Attendance with the Crown Prince[1]

The dazzling sun shines through a clear sky,
the seasonal rains having laid to rest the flowing dust.
The ice has dispelled the gathering heat,
my body is cooled by the breeze.
The golden goblets are brimming with clear wine,
delicacies spread across the table.
The ladies of Qi serve up their peculiar music,
and girls from Qin present their songs.
My prince, how gracefully he conducts himself,
suddenly his skills seem to have fallen straight from heaven.

---

1 此处的太子是曹丕。The "Crown Prince" here refers to Cao Pi, Cao Zhi's elder brother.

野田黄雀行

高树多悲风,
海水扬其波。
利剑不在掌,
结友何须多?
不见篱间雀,
见鹞自投罗。
罗家得雀喜,
少年见雀悲。
拔剑捎罗网,
黄雀得飞飞。
飞飞摩苍天,
来下谢少年。

A Yellow Sparrow in the Wild Fields

The wind mourns in the treetops,
the sea is lifting its waves.
No sword in my hand,
why do I need many friends?
See there, the sparrow, catching sight of the circling eagle,
flaps from the hedgerow into the waiting net.
The trapper dances in delight
but seeing the bird, the young boy is sad.
With a sudden thrust he cuts the cords
and the sparrow takes to the sky;
he lifts, then soars, to the edge of heaven,
down he swoops again, to thank the boy.

杂诗

高台多悲风,
朝日照北林。
之子在万里,
江湖迥且深。
方舟安可极,
离思故难任。
孤雁飞南游,
过庭长哀吟。
翘思慕远人,
愿欲托遗音。
形影忽不见,
翩翩伤我心。

Poem

A sorrowful wind crosses the high pavilion,
the morning sun glitters through the northern wood.
You are now ten thousand *li* from me
where the rivers are long and lakes are deep.
Our boats cannot get to touch prow to prow,
the pain of separation is too much to bear.
A lonely goose is flying south and
passing the courtyard keening his loss.
Craning my neck I long for you who are far away
and beg this bird to carry my lingering song.
All of a sudden its shadow is gone from sight,
as it flaps its wings, leaving me in sorrow.

盘石篇

盘盘山巅石,
飘飖涧底蓬。
我本泰山人,
何为客淮东?
蒹葭弥斥土,
林木无芬重。
岸岩若崩缺,
湖水何汹汹。
蚌蛤被滨涯,
光采如锦虹。
高波凌云霄,
浮气象螭龙。
鲸脊若丘陵,
须若山上松。
呼吸吞船栅,
澎濞戏中鸿。
方舟寻高价,
珍宝丽以通。
一举必千里,
乘飓举帆幢。
经危履险阻,
未知命所钟。

The Great Rock

See a boulder, high on the mountain top,
and the floating grass at the bottom of the valley.
I, by birth, am a man of Mount Tai,
so what keeps me here at Huaidong?
The reeds are sprouting, covering the salty soil
and trees don't flourish here.
The rocks are broken, jagged,
and waves clash in the lake.
Clamshells all over the shore,
blinding, overwrought brocade.
Now the waves rise higher, cloudwards,
air currents buckle like hornless dragons,
whalebacks swell like mountains,
their whiskers bristle like hilltop pines.
With a breath, such a whale may swallow a ship,
and blowing its nose, its spray will dance with the gulls.
Taking a boat, I search for the precious things,
donning all the necessary jewelry to ease my travels.
Once begun, I must journey a thousand *li*
and pressing forward, sails set high in the powerful wind,
face every danger, meet obstructions,
the course of my fate unknown.

常恐沉黄垆,
下与鼋鳖同。
南极苍梧野,
游盼穷九江。
中夜指参辰,
欲师当定从。
仰天长太息,
思想怀故邦。
乘桴何所志,
吁嗟我孔公!

Often, I am afraid I'll only sink in the dust
and degenerate into a friend of turtle and fish.
Heading south I will reach the Cangwu wilderness
and cast my gaze over the Nine Rivers.
At midnight I point at Shen and Chen, two opposing stars,
time to decide which one to follow.
Holding my head I sigh to the sky,
heartsick for home.
Boarding a raft, but which direction would he take?
Alas, our Master Confucius![1]

1　孔子曾说过:"道不行,乘桴游于海。" Confucius once said, "If the Way does not prevail, I would board a raft and float on the sea."

仙人篇

仙人揽六著,
对博太山隅。
湘娥拊琴瑟,
秦女吹笙竽。
玉樽盈桂酒,
河伯献神鱼。
四海一何局,
九州安所如?
韩终与王乔,
要我于天衢。
万里不足步,
轻举凌太虚。
飞腾逾景云,
高风吹我躯。
回驾观紫微,
与帝合灵符。
阊阖正嵯峨,
双阙万丈余。

The Immortals

The immortals were playing chess
down at the corner of Mount Tai.
The river nymphs were playing their zithers,
and the girl of Qin was singing the songs for the lute.
Jade cups were full to the lip with osmanthus wine
and the God of the Yellow River presented a supernatural fish!
These Four Seas: they're more like a prison to me,
where is there left worth seeing in all the Nine States?[1]
Han Zhong and Wang Ziqiao, themselves immortals,
asked me to travel with them along the Heavenly Path.
Lightly we soar through heaven,
ten thousand *li* in a single step.
We hover above the colorful clouds,
my body drifts on the high wind.
Heading back, we view the palace of the Heavenly God,
and match our tally with his.
The celestial gate stands majestically tall,
its double towers are ten-thousand feet.

---

1 古代中国人认为中国以外四方皆有海围绕。九州即指中国。The ancient Chinese believed that beyond the Chinese nation there were four seas in each direction. "Nine States" is another name for China.

玉树扶道生,
白虎夹门枢。
驱风游四海,
东过王母庐。
俯观五岳间,
人生如寄居。
潜光养羽翼,
进趋且徐徐。
不见轩辕氏,
乘龙出鼎湖。
徘徊九天上,
与尔长相须。

Jade trees blossom along the paths,
white tigers crouching in every doorway.
Thus we traverse the Four Seas, riding the back of the wind,
heading eastward, passing the hut of Queen Mother,
 the goddess,
looking down on the Five Great Peaks on earth:
human life is just like a mere moment's stay.
Withdrawing into seclusion, we cultivate our wings,
and swinging them back, then forward, with serenity.
Don't you see the Yellow Emperor
who rose on a dragon from the Tripod Lake?[1]
We also roam the Nine Skies
and await his arrival, forever.

---

1 据传说，黄帝在鼎湖乘龙升天。According to legend, the Yellow Emperor was taken to heaven by a dragon at Tripod Lake.

游仙

人生不满百,
岁岁少欢娱。
意欲奋六翮,
排雾凌紫虚。
蝉蜕同松乔,
翻迹登鼎湖。
翱翔九天上,
骋辔远行游。
东观扶桑曜,
西临弱水流。
北极玄天渚,
南翔陟丹丘。

A Trip to Join the Immortals

Our life is not a hundred years long,
the years come and go and give so little pleasure!
I wish I had wings, six golden wings,
and clearing the fog about me, head up straight to heaven.
Like Song and Qiao,[1] I'd give up this old cicada shell
and sail through the sky to the great Tripod Lake.
I'd hover in the Ninth Heaven, where sky ends;
then ride and ride on horseback
to the East: to gaze on where the sun comes up,
to the West: to stand up straight where it sets,
to the North: to attain the Dark Isle,
to the South: I would climb the Red Hill
　　　　—these the homes of the gods.

1　松、乔，即赤松子、王子乔，传说中的仙人。Song and Qiao refer to Chi Songzi and Wang Ziqiao, who are legendary immortals.

升天行（二首）

其一

乘蹻追术士，
远之蓬莱山。
灵液飞素波，
兰桂上参天。
玄豹游其下，
翔鹍戏其巅。
乘风忽登举，
仿佛见众仙。

其二

扶桑之所出，
乃在朝阳溪。
中心凌苍昊，
布叶盖天涯。
日出登东干，
既夕没西枝。
愿得纡阳辔，
回日使东驰。

A Trip to Heaven (two Poems)

1

Lifted by charm, I am chasing the magicians
to Penglai Mountain, the home of the gods!
Streams fall, pure nectar-streams,
and cassia trees are rising high, as high as heaven.
Black leopards swim at the mountain's foot
and at its peak, phoenixes are playing.
I am hanging on the wind, and suddenly flying upwards,
a cloud of gods and goddesses come into sight!

2

Fusang, where the sun comes up,
look for it by the sunshine stream.
Its central part clings to the blue sky,
leaves spreading to the end of heaven.
The sun climbs up the eastern boughs,
descends the western branches.
I wish I could hold the Sun-cart's reins,
and pivot it back to the east!

七步诗

煮豆持作羹,
漉豉以为汁。
萁在釜下燃,
豆在釜中泣。
本是同根生,
相煎何太急?

The Seven-step Poem

People boil beans to make bean curd,
they sieve soya to make a drink.
The beanstalk burns beneath the pot
and beans in the pot cry out.
Born as they are of the selfsame root,
why should one torment the other?

应诏

肃承明诏,
应会皇都。
星陈凤驾,
秣马脂车。
命彼掌徒,
肃我征旅。
朝发鸾台,
夕宿兰渚。
芒芒原隰,
祁祁士女。
经彼公田,
乐我稷黍。
爰有樛木,
重阴匪息。
虽有糇粮,
饥不遑食。
望城不过,
面邑不游。
仆夫警策,
平路是由。
玄驷蔼蔼,
扬镳漂沫。
流风翼衡,

At Imperial Command

Solemnly I received the enlightened command
to attend an audience in the imperial capital.
I had the carriage yoked by starlight,
the horses fed and the wheels greased.
I ordered the clerks in charge
to make provision for my journey.
At dawn we set out from the Crane Terrace,
by dusk we reached the Orchid Marsh.
The plains and wetlands were vast before us,
men and women thriving.
We rode past government lands
and were delighted to see the abundant crops.
The branches on the trees bent low
but, despite their shade, we did not rest.
We had brought plenty of food for the road,
but we did not pause to eat, despite our hunger.
We beheld the cities, but chose not enter them,
the towns, we chose not to visit them.
My drivers whipped up the horses,
they only followed the level roads.
Four black horses, galloping in line,
raising their bits, and blowing out froth!
The wind pressed the carriage forward,

轻云承盖。
涉涧之滨,
缘山之隈。
遵彼河浒,
黄坂是阶。
西济关谷,
或降或升。
騑骖倦路,
载寝载兴。
将朝圣皇,
匪敢晏宁。
弭节长骛,
指日遄征。
前驱举燧,
后乘抗旌。
轮不辍运,
鸾无废声。
爰暨帝室,
税此西墉。
嘉诏未赐,
朝觐莫从。
仰瞻城阈,
俯惟阙庭。
长怀永慕,
忧心如酲。

light clouds, hanging above its canopy.
We journeyed along the valley streams,
and trailed past mountain nooks.
We followed the banks of the river,
and climbed those yellow slopes.
Westward, we bridged passes and ravines,
downwards, upwards, onwards we pressed.
When the horses were exhausted,
we rested briefly, then were quickly back on the road.
On my way to pay my respects to the Emperor,
I dared not take my rest or ease.
Only stopping briefly, we raced along,
always trying to cover more miles every day.
The vanguards lifted their flags,
the rearguards raised their banners.
The wheels never ceased from turning,
the simurg bells from singing.
When we finally reached the imperial palace,
I was put up out by the western wall.
The auspicious summon has not come,
and I cannot pay my respects at court.
Looking up, I can see the palace gate,
looking down, I imagine the court.
I cherish my eternal longing,
but I am anxious, as if my heart is sick with drinking.

赠白马王彪

黄初四年五月,白马王、任城王与余俱朝京师,会节气。到洛阳,任城王薨。至七月,与白马王还国。后有司以二王归藩,道路宜异宿止。意毒恨之。盖以大别在数日,是用自剖,与王辞焉,愤而成篇。

其一

谒帝承明庐,
逝将归旧疆。
清晨发皇邑,
日夕过首阳。
伊洛广且深,
欲济川无梁。
泛舟越洪涛,
怨彼东路长。
顾瞻恋城阙,
引领情内伤。

To Cao Biao, the Prince of Baima

The Princes of Baima and Rencheng and myself attended the Imperial Presence together in the fifth month of the fourth year of Huangchu (AD 233) for the promulgation of the calendar. Prince Rencheng died on reaching Luoyang, and Prince Baima and I left for home in the seventh month, but the official thought that when two princes returned to their places they must take separate ways and not travel together. I bitterly resented this. As we were bound to part in a few days, I penned this poem in anger to express my feelings and to bid farewell to the prince.

1

Having paid our respects to the Emperor,
we departed for our separate fiefdoms.
We rode out of the capital at dawn,
as evening fell we were passing Mount Shouyang.
The Yi and the Luo were deep and wide,
no bridge to bear us across as we hope.
We took a boat and fought the torrential waves,
and we resented, endless the eastern road.
I looked back at the city as it disappeared,
and raised my head to it in sorrow.

其二

太谷何寥廓,
山树郁苍苍。
霖雨泥我涂,
流潦浩纵横。
中逵绝无轨,
改辙登高岗。
修坂造云日,
我马玄以黄。

2

How vast the valley of Taigu,
and lush the trees and the mountains.
Rain made mud of the path
and mire of the lands.
The roads became completely blocked,
so we turned to the track of the high hillsides
and the long slope up to the clouds;
      beyond the clouds, the sun.
My horse dizzy, staggering.

其三

玄黄犹能进,
我思郁以纡。
郁纡将何念?
亲爱在离居。
本图相与偕,
中更不克俱。
鸱枭鸣衡轭,
豺狼当路衢。
苍蝇间白黑,
谗巧令亲疏。
欲还绝无蹊,
揽辔止踟蹰。

3

Dizzy, staggering, still we go on,
my heart knotted in sorrow.
Knotted in sorrow, what is in my mind?
brothers are parting, one from another.
I thought I might be company for you,
but halfway there things took a wrong turn.
Sinister owls are whooping before my cart
and ravenous wolves obstruct the path.
Flies turn black to white and white to black
and slander separates friends and relations.
I want to turn again, but there is no road,
I hesitate, my hand upon the bridle.

其四

踟蹰亦何留,
相思无终极。
秋风发微凉,
寒蝉鸣我侧。
原野何萧条,
白日忽西匿。
归鸟赴乔林,
翩翩厉羽翼。
孤兽走索群,
衔草不遑食。
感物伤我怀,
抚心长太息。

4

I hesitate: what is it that I long for?
My love for you feels limitless.
Now the autumn wind brings chill,
and a shivering cicada chirrups at my side.
So desolate is this wilderness,
the bright sun suddenly extinguished in the west.
The birds hurry past me, home to the treetops,
with urgent, widespread wings.
A lonely animal snuffles for its companions,
grass in mouth, no time to swallow.
My heart is grieved to find itself in such a place.
Hand on my chest, a lengthy sigh escapes me.

其五

太息将何为?
天命与我违。
奈何念同生,
一往形不归。
孤魂翔故域,
灵柩寄京师。
存者忽复过,
亡没身自衰。
人生处一世,
去若朝露晞。
年在桑榆间,
影响不能追。
自顾非金石,
咄唶令心悲。

5

But what's the use of sighing?
Providence dictates against my fate.
I think of the brother
who'll never return in bodily form.
His lonely ghost hovers around the old place,
while his coffin lies in the capital.
Those still living walk quickly past,
the lifeless body swiftly falls apart.
Man's life on earth is brief
as the morning dew that dries so quick.
Our year has reached Sang and Yu, where the sun sets,
and we can never catch its shadow, or its sounds.
As for myself, I am no metal ore,
and thus my heart is grieved.

其六

心悲动我神,
弃置莫复陈。
丈夫志四海,
万里犹比邻。
恩爱苟不亏,
在远分日亲。
何必同衾帱,
然后展殷勤。
忧思成疾疢,
无乃儿女仁。
仓卒骨肉情,
能不怀苦辛?

6

My heart is grieved and so my soul,
let's end it there, not harp on such complaints.
A man can exert his will across the entire Four Seas,
separated by ten thousand *li* we are still neighbors.
If our affections do not decline,
the further away, the tighter the bonds.
We don't need to share the same silk cover
to show the intimacy of our love.
Too much depression will hurt our health
and all this moaning sentimental, childish.
Yet as the bone and flesh of the selfsame body are ripped apart,
how can we not feel our anguish?

其七

苦辛何虑思?
天命信可疑。
虚无求列仙,
松子久吾欺。
变故在斯须,
百年谁能持?
离别永无会,
执手将何时?
王其爱玉体,
俱享黄发期。
收泪即长路,
援笔从此辞。

7

This anguish though, where is its reason?
Providence is indeed full of doubt.
In the middle of nowhere I seek the immortals,
one, Songzi, has deceived me constantly.
The unexpected happens every minute,
who can expect to live a hundred years?
Once parted, we can never be reunited,
when will we clasp hands again?
Your Honor: take care of your body of jade!
Together we'll enjoy the time of grey hair.
A long road lies ahead of us, I hold my tears.
Pen in hand, I take my leave.

浮萍篇

浮萍寄清水,
随风东西流。
结发辞严亲,
来为君子仇。
恪勤在朝夕,
无端获罪尤。
在昔蒙恩惠,
和乐如瑟琴。
何意今摧颓,
旷若商与参。
茱萸自有芳,
不若桂与兰。
新人虽可爱,
不若故人欢。
行云有反期,
君恩倘中还?
慊慊仰天叹,
愁心将何诉?
日月不恒处,
人生忽若寓。

On Duckweed

Duckweed lives on top of clear river water,
drifts with the wind, to the east, to the west.
At age 15, I put up my hair and bade farewell to my parents,
I came to be your bride my lord.
I toiled from morning to evening,
only to get a scolding for no cause.
While I was still held high in your esteem,
we were happy as flute and zither played in tune.
Now I am past my prime,
you treat us like enemies.
Yes, dogwood does have its fragrance,
but can't be compared with laurel or violet.
Your new wife may be beautiful,
but still she's not as pleasing as the old.
And like the floating cloud has its time of return,
so may your favor?
I hold my face to the sky, in mourning,
where's the relief for a mournful heart?
The sun and moon cannot stay forever
and human life is just like a brief sojourn.

悲风来入帷,
泪下如垂露。
散箧造新衣,
裁缝纨与素。

Sorrowful the breeze that billows inside the curtain,
and like falling dew, my tears.
I take down my sewing box to stitch new clothes for myself,
cut from the shiniest satin, the finest silk.

七哀

明月照高楼,
流光正徘徊。
上有愁思妇,
悲叹有余哀。
借问叹者谁,
言是宕子妻。
君行逾十年,
孤妾常独栖。
君若清路尘,
妾若浊水泥。
浮沉各异势,
会合何时谐?
愿为西南风,
长逝入君怀。
君怀良不开,
贱妾当何依?

Seven Sorrows

The moon gleams on the high pavilion,
its light flowing, shimmering.
There, high on the pavilion, see a woman,
sighing mournfully, enduring her sorrow.
Ask who she is, the one who endlessly sighs.
She is one whose husband is far from home.
> "My lord has been absent for a good ten years,
> and all this time I have led my lonely life.
> My lord, you are like the light dust on the road,
> your woman the silt in dirty water.
> Rising and sinking, they have their ways,
> but when can they unite in harmony?
> I'd like to be the southwest wind
> and flow into your breast, my lord.
> But your breast would not open.
> What is there left to rely on, for a humble woman?"

种葛篇

种葛南山下,
葛藟自成阴。
与君初婚时,
结发恩义深。
欢爱在枕席,
宿昔同衣衾。
窃慕棠棣篇,
好乐和瑟琴。
行年将晚暮,
佳人怀异心。
恩纪旷不接,
我情遂抑沉。
出门当何顾?
徘徊步北林。
下有交颈兽,
仰见双栖禽。
攀枝长叹息,
泪下沾罗衿。
良马知我悲,
延颈对我吟。
昔为同池鱼,
今为商与参。

On Planting the Kudzu Vine

Kudzu vines are planted at the foot of southern hill,
their branches twine together, casting a shadow.
When we were newly wed and my hair
was braided so, our youthful love was deep.
We took our pleasure from the mat and the pillow,
morning and evening sharing the same cover and clothes;
we whispered an ancient love song,
happy as lute and zither sweetly played in tune.
Now I'm getting old
my loved one owns a foreign heart.
His favor is over,
my heart has sunk.
I walk out, but what to look for?
I wander through the northern woods.
Beneath there are animals twining their necks,
up in the treetops, the birds are coupling.
I cling to a branch and give out a long sigh,
tears dampen my silken sleeves.
My faithful horse, he understands my sorrow,
and rubs his neck against me, murmuring.
Once we were fishes, sharing the pond,
now we are the opposite stars.

往古皆欢遇,
我独困于今。
弃置委天命,
悠悠安可任?

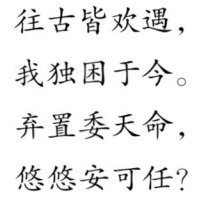

Since ancient time people all treasure company,
today I stand alone in my loneliness.
Forget it all, just follow the road of providence,
so vast and long its path,
> could I endure the journey?

喜雨

天覆何弥广，
苞育此群生。
弃之必憔悴，
惠之则滋荣。
庆云从北来，
郁述西南征。
时雨终夜降，
长雷周我廷。
嘉种盈膏壤，
登秋必有成。

Delighted by Rain

How wide the canopy of heaven,
it nourishes all living things.
Without the rain, they all wither,
Favored by it, they would thrive.
Auspicious clouds come from the north,
densely they make their way southwest.
The rain arrives on time and falls all night,
while thunder lingers around the court.
Let's plant seeds in the richly moistened field,
and wait for the reward of autumn's harvest!

杂诗

仆夫早严驾,
吾行将远游。
远游欲何之?
吴国为我仇。
将骋万里涂,
东路安足由?
江介多悲风,
淮泗驰急流。
愿欲一轻济,
惜哉无方舟。
闲居非吾志,
甘心赴国忧。

Poem

My driver brings my carriage round at dawn
for we will have a long way to travel.
Where am I going, so far away?
The kingdom of my enemy, the Wu.
We will gallop for thousands of *li* and more,
the eastern road is unworthy of our team.
Many the sorrowful winds that billow along the rivers,
the Huai and the Si flow fast.
I wish for a crossing easy and light,
what a shame there's no boat to be found!
To lead a leisurely life is not my will,
I'd rather fight to ease my country's woe.

鰕䱇篇

鰕䱇游潢潦,
不知江海流。
燕雀戏藩柴,
安识鸿鹄游?
世士此诚明,
大德固无俦。
驾言登五岳,
然后小陵丘。
俯观上路人,
势利惟是谋。
高念翼皇家,
远怀柔九州。
抚剑而雷音,
猛气纵横浮。
泛泊徒嗷嗷,
谁知壮士忧?

The Fish and the Eel

The fish and the eel swim in rain water,
oblivious to the flow of river and ocean.
Sparrows and swallows play in hedgerows,
how can they know of the swan's soaring?
The world's scholars understand this truth,
great virtue is beyond comparison.
Go, climb the very summit of Mount Tai,
and then consider the hills, how small they seem.
Look, down there, those people, flowing up and down
    the road,
power and wealth their only goal.
My own ideal is to assist our Emperor
and to devote myself to pacifying the country.
I hold my sword aloft! The crash of storm resounds!
my noble spirit permeates the universe!
The philistines that prattle loud and vain,
who among them understands the hero's concerns?

吁嗟篇

吁嗟此转蓬,
居世何独然!
长去本根逝,
宿夜无休闲。
东西经七陌,
南北越九阡。
卒遇回风起,
吹我入云间。
自谓终天路,
忽然下沉泉。
惊飙接我出,
故归彼中田。
当南而更北,
谓东而反西。
宕宕当何依,
忽亡而复存。
飘飘周八泽,
连翩历五山。
流转无恒处,
谁知吾苦艰?

Alas

Alas! This uprooted tumbleweed,
how lonely its life on this earth.
"Once I have split from my root
day and night I cannot find my place,
east and west, I cross seven roads,
and south and north, nine paths.
until at last I collide with a whirlwind,
which blasts me into the clouds!
I thought I would reach the end of the heavenly path,
but then I fell, and smashed into an abyss.
Then came a gale, lifting me out of the water
and tossed me back to a field.
I set off south, but found myself traveling north,
Wait! I was on my way east, not west!
Floating all over, what's left for me to rely on?
I'm utterly lost, but then come to myself again;
then another gust, lifting me over eight moors,
and sending me flying across five mountains.
Drifting, drifting, with no place to land,
who can know the hardship of this life?

愿为中林草,
秋随野火燔。
糜灭岂不痛,
愿与株荄连。

I wish I were the grass which springs in the forest.
Scorched by autumn forest fires,
its pain and suffering cannot be denied,
but still I'd be connected to my root."

美女篇

美女妖且闲,
采桑歧路间。
柔条纷冉冉,
落叶何翩翩。
攘袖见素手,
皓腕约金环。
头上金爵钗,
腰佩翠琅玕。
明珠交玉体,
珊瑚间木难。
罗衣何飘飘,
轻裾随风还。
顾盼遗光彩,
长啸气若兰。
行徒用息驾,
休者以忘餐。
借问女何居,
乃在城南端。
青楼临大路,
高门结重关。

On a Beautiful Woman

Such charm, such physical grace, and beauty!
Standing at the crossroads, plucking mulberry leaves.
The tender boughs bob up and down
and the leaves falling, endlessly falling around her.
Her sleeves ride up, reveal the whiteness of her hands,
her shining wrists, encircled with gold.
See, a golden swallow has landed in her hair—a pin!
her waist is wrapped in green agate.
Lustrous pearls adorn this body of jade,
coral pearls and lapis lazuli!
A silken robe drifts around her,
Her skirt is floating on the breeze.
Now she glances back: the light, the color from her eyes!
And she lets out a long, soft whistle on her breath
                that is fragranced with violets.
Carts and horses are brought to a halt,
and resting workers gape, forgetting to eat their food.
"May we ask where this lady lives?"
"At the southern end of the town,
in a tall green mansion that faces the road,
whose door is fastened with double bolts."

容华耀朝日,
谁不希令颜?
媒氏何所营,
玉帛不时安。
佳人慕高义,
求贤良独难。
众人徒嗷嗷,
安知彼所观?
盛年处房室,
中夜起长叹。

Her face graces the morning sun,
who can look, without longing, upon it?
What are the matchmakers playing at?
Why are the jade and silk not arrayed in time?
A noble mind will look for noble virtue,
to find a virtuous man is no easy task.
People may vainly gossip and slander,
but how can they begin to understand her dreams?
In the prime of life she is forced to stay at home,
pacing the boards at midnight, she sighs her long sighs.

杂诗

南国有佳人,
容华若桃李。
朝游江北岸,
夕宿潇湘沚。
时俗薄朱颜,
谁为发皓齿?
俯仰岁将暮,
荣耀难久恃。

Poem

Down south there lives a pretty woman,
fair of face as pear or plum flowers.
Mornings find her roaming north of the Yangtze,
evenings she rests on an isle in the Xiang.
It is the time's custom to scorn her beauty,
for whom shall she open her jade-white teeth and sing?
A nod of the head and she grows as old as evening,
O hard, for beauty and glory to last.

杂诗

转蓬离本根,
飘飖随长风。
何意回飙举,
吹我入云中。
高高上无极,
天路安可穷?
类此游客子,
捐躯远从戎。
毛褐不掩形,
薇藿常不充。
去去莫复道,
沉忧令人老。

Poem

The tumbleweed is torn from its root,
takes flight on the long wind.
Why should this tempest uproot me,
casting me into the clouds
and higher, through limitless skies?
How can we reach the end of the heavenly path?
Such is the life of those who, far from home,
give up their lives to fight for their country.
Their shabby clothes can barely cover them,
the bean leaves they eat are never enough.
Yet let us leave this talk!
Such deep worries make one old!

五游

九州不足步,
愿得凌云翔。
逍遥八纮外,
游目历遐荒。
披我丹霞衣,
袭我素霓裳。
华盖芬晻蔼,
六龙仰天骧。
曜灵未移景,
倏忽造昊苍。
阊阖启丹扉,
双阙曜朱光。
徘徊文昌殿,
登陟太微堂。
上帝休西棂,
群后集东厢。
带我琼瑶佩,
漱我沆瀣浆。
踟蹰玩灵芝,
徙倚弄华芳。

A Journey in the Fifth Direction

Even the length and breadth of earth cramps my stride,
so I wanted to journey, just like a cloud, to the highest
    heaven;
there I may roam at ease, beyond the edges of the earth
and cast my eyes across infinite wilderness.
Clad in celestial robes,
donned in rainbow clothing,
my chariot's painted canopy bright between thick clouds
as six dragons haul me heavenwards.
The sun has not even moved its shadow
and I find myself already in space;
the heavenly gate's crimson doors swing open,
whose double towers radiate rosy light.
I'm strolling around the Wenchang Temple,
and ascending the Taiwei Hall.
The Heavenly God is leaning on his west window,
his retinue assemble in the east room.
And me? Decked in amber pendants,
drinking the dew of midnight air,
I wander up and down, twirling the magical mushrooms,
I wander up and down, admiring the beautiful flowers.

王子奉仙药,
羡门进奇方,
服食享遐纪,
延寿保无疆。

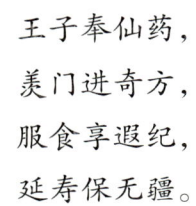

The immortal Wang Ziqiao brings celestial medicine,
Xian Men, another god, offers exotic prescriptions.
Take, and eat, this food of longevity!
Accept this dish of eternal life!

远游篇

远游临四海,
俯仰观洪波。
大鱼若曲陵,
乘浪相经过。
灵鳌戴方丈,
神岳俨嵯峨。
仙人翔其隅,
玉女戏其阿。
琼蕊可疗饥,
仰首吸朝霞。
昆仑本吾宅,
中州非我家。
将归谒东父,
一举超流沙。
鼓翼舞时风,
长啸激清歌。
金石固易弊,
日月同光华。
齐年与天地,
万乘安足多!

A Journey to a Distant Land

I traveled a great distance to the end of Four Seas,
watched the huge waves up and down as they swell,
saw fish as big as folded hills
riding the waves, passing and repassing one another.
Divine turtles carried the godly mountain,
so grand to the eye, magnificent!
Immortals hovered at each foot of the mountain,
fairy women played among its slopes.
They eased their hunger with magic plants,
and stretched their throats to drink the dewy morning clouds.
Mount Kunlun: this is my own original place,
central China is not my home.
I want to return to Eastern Father the god,
to fly across the floating desert,
spread my wings to the season's wind,
and loudly sing my pure, clear songs!
Metal and stone after all are easy to break,
the brilliance of the sun and moon shines forever.
An eternal life equals heaven and earth,
it shames a kingdom of ten thousand chariots.

泰山梁甫行

八方各异气,
千里殊风雨。
剧哉边海民,
寄身于草墅。
妻子象禽兽,
行止依林阻。
柴门何萧条,
狐兔翔我宇。

A Liang Fu Song at Mount Tai

Each of the Eight Directions has its own climate,
even the wind and rain feel different a thousand *li* away.
Life is hard for the sea-coast folk:
they make their living from the wilderness,
their wives and children are like beasts,
they are the slaves of barren forest and hills.
How desolate these wicket gates!
Foxes and rabbits hanging around the house.

白马篇

白马饰金羁,
连翩西北驰。
借问谁家子,
幽并游侠儿。
少小去乡邑,
扬声沙漠垂。
宿昔秉良弓,
楛矢何参差。
控弦破左的,
右发摧月支。
仰手接飞猱,
俯身散马蹄。
狡捷过猴猿,
勇剽若豹螭。
边城多警急,
虏骑数迁移。
羽檄从北来,
厉马登高堤。
长驱蹈匈奴,
左顾陵鲜卑。

The White Horse

See a white horse in a golden halter
galloping fast northwest.
Ask which family's son is its rider:
a brave knight, who hails from Youbing.
He left his home in early youth, and now
knows fame throughout the deserts.
Morning and evening he clutches his bow
and bunches of arrows swing from his sides.
He pulls his bow—the left-hand target is pierced,
he shoots at the right and cuts another through.
Upwards his arrows seek out the flying apes,
downwards they shatter the horseshoe target.
His dexterity even surpasses the monkeys,
his courage the leopard, or even the hornless dragon!
Alarms are heard from the frontier!
northern tribesmen are pouring into the country,
feathered war-letters fly from the north.
Reining his horse, he clambers the highest hill
then charges, to the right, the Xiongnu troops,
then, to the left, the army of Xianbei.[1]

---

1 匈奴、鲜卑是当时居住于边疆地区的少数民族。Xiongnu and Xianbei were people living in the border regions.

弃身锋刃端，
性命安可怀？
父母且不顾，
何言子与妻！
名在壮士籍，
不得中顾私。
捐躯赴国难，
视死忽如归。

He's staked himself on the edge of his sword,
how can he treasure his own existence?
Even his parents are put to the back of his thoughts,
let alone his children and his wife.
If his name is to be written in the roll of the heroes,
he can't be concerned with his own well-being.
He offers his life for the sake of his country.
He looks on death as a journey home.

豫章行(二首)

其一

穷达难豫图,
祸福信亦然。
虞舜不逢尧,
耕耘处中田。
太公未遭文,
渔钓终渭川。
不见鲁孔丘,
穷困陈蔡间?
周公下白屋,
天下称其贤。

A Yu Zhang Song (two poems)

1

Poverty and wealth can't be foreseen,
neither can luck or misfortune.
Shun, if hadn't met Yao the King,[1]
would have stayed all his life a peasant.
Lord Jiang, if he hadn't impressed King Wen,[2]
would have ended up fishing the Wei River.
Didn't you just see that Confucius of Lu
trapped in his difficulties at Chen and Cai?
Duke Zhou paid due respect to humble scholars
and all under heaven praised his virtue.

---

1 尧、舜皆为传说中的领袖。尧选舜为他的继承人。Yao and Shun are legendary rulers. Yao chose Shun to be his successor.
2 太公，即吕尚。他曾在渭水边垂钓，被周文王发现，并被任为大臣。Lord Jiang was once fishing by the Wei River; he was discovered and appointed a minister by King Wen of the Zhou Dynasty.

其二

鸳鸯自朋亲,
不若比翼连。
他人虽同盟,
骨肉天性然。
周公穆康叔,
管蔡则流言。
子臧让千乘,
季札慕其贤。

2

Mandarin ducks live out their lives in faithful pairs,
but even they can't be compared with the Biyi birds.[1]
People may form alliances with each other,
but only the bone and flesh are connected by nature.
The Duke of Zhou showed affections to Kangshu,
but Guanshu and Caishu spread slanders against him.[2]
Zizang declined the kingdom of ten thousand carts—
his virtue earned him the admiration of Jizha.[3]

---

1 有关比翼鸟，参见《送应氏·其二》注。For Biyi birds, see the note to the second poem of "Two Valedictions for Mr. Ying."
2 康叔、管叔和蔡叔皆为周公的弟弟。此事又见于《怨歌行》。Kangshu, Guanshu and Caishu were all brothers of the Duke of Zhou. This story was also told in his "Song of Complaint."
3 子臧、季札皆为春秋时代人物。子臧曾谢绝吴国的君位，受到季札的赞赏。Zizang and Jizha are historical figures during the Spring and Autumn period. Zizang once declined to be the ruler of Wu, which won the admiration from Jizha.

薤露行

天地无穷极,
阴阳转相因。
人居一世间,
忽若风吹尘。
愿得展功勤,
输力于明君。
怀此王佐才,
慷慨独不群。
鳞介尊神龙,
走兽宗麒麟。
虫兽犹知德,
何况于士人。
孔氏删诗书,
王业粲已分。
骋我径寸翰,
流藻垂华芬。

Dew on the Leek

Heaven and earth are beyond us,
Yin and Yang change over.
Human life in this world
is like dust blown away by a sudden wind.
I'd like to put my skills
in our enlightened ruler's hands.
This ability to help his majesty
makes a true hero outstanding.
Fishes, with their shiny scaly skin,
    worship their god the Dragon,
and every galloping beast on earth
    exalts the Unicorn.
Even animals and insects know this virtue,
let alone our most learned scholars.
Confucius edited the classics of Poetry and History,
outlining the splendid deeds of ancient kings.
Now it's up to me to take my inch-wide brush
to bequeath in rainbow words the glory of our cause!

箜篌引

置酒高殿上,
亲友从我游。
中厨办丰膳,
烹羊宰肥牛。
秦筝何慷慨,
齐瑟和且柔。
阳阿奏奇舞,
京洛出名讴。
乐饮过三爵,
缓带倾庶羞。
主称千金寿,
宾奉万年酬。
久要不可忘,
薄终义所尤。
谦谦君子德,
磬折欲何求?
惊风飘白日,
光景驰西流。
盛时不再来,
百年忽我遒。

Song to Accompany the *Kong Hou*

Wine is set in the high halls,

relatives and friends enjoy themselves in my company.

The cooks are toiling in the kitchen for the feast,

they're boiling lambs and killing fattened cows.

The music of the Qin zither is heroic,

the Qi harp soft and harmonious.

The Yang'e dancers go through their peculiar steps,

the Luoyang singers sing their famous songs.

Three rounds of wine have passed, and the guests

loosen their belts for the finest dishes.

The host gives out a thousand treasures to his guests,

and they answer him with "life of ten thousand years!"

This vow, we swear, should never be forgotten,

eating one's words is what friendship condemns.

Modesty and courtesy are the gentleman's virtues,

what traits apart from these could we possibly desire?

A gale arises, blowing the bright sun, and

shifting its brilliance to the west.

Time of prosperity cannot be repeated,

a hundred years suddenly stare in my face.

生存华屋处,
零落归山丘。
先民谁不死,
知命复何忧?

Alive, we dwell in magnificent houses,

dead, we return to the hills.

Our ancestors all have passed away,

and if we knew our fates what terror would they hold?

名都篇

名都多妖女,
京洛出少年。
宝剑直千金,
被服丽且鲜。
斗鸡东郊道,
走马长楸间。
驰骋未能半,
双兔过我前。
揽弓捷鸣镝,
长驱上南山。
左挽因右发,
一纵两禽连。
余巧未及展,
仰手接飞鸢。
观者咸称善,
众工归我妍。
我归宴平乐,
美酒斗十千。
脍鲤臇胎鰕,
炮鳖炙熊蹯。
鸣俦啸匹侣,
列坐竟长筵。

On the Renowned Cities

The renowned cities teem with beautiful women,
and Luoyang, the capital, with fine-looking youths.
Their swords alone are worth thousands in gold,
their clothes are brilliant, luxurious.
In the eastern suburb they gather around to watch cockfights,
their horses prance the length of the avenue.
Halfway through the ride
two rabbits scurry in front of me.
Waving my bow to the sky, I unsheathe a sounding arrow
and gallop straight up southern hill.
Left hand on the bow, I pull to shoot with the right,
and both of the rabbits are killed with a single shot!
I've still to show off my other abilities:
See! I shot down a hawk in flight!
Everyone there cheers,
my fellow huntsmen praise my skill.
Upon our return, we banquet at Pingle Palace,
on the finest wine and ten thousand delicacies:
shredded carp meat, fish curd in broth,
and grilled turtle, fried bear paw …
My boisterous comrades shout to one another,
sitting together they stretch the length of the mat.

连翩击鞠壤，
巧捷惟万端。
白日西南驰，
光景不可攀。
云散还城邑，
清晨复来还。

They play the ballgame with incredible dexterity,

sharp their skill, and dazzling!

Southwest speeds the sun

and nothing can hold its light.

The young men leave the party like clouds dispersing,

agreeing to gather again, the following day.

杂诗

西北有织妇,
绮缟何缤纷。
明晨秉机杼,
日昃不成文。
太息终长夜,
悲啸入青云。
妾身守空闺,
良人行从军。
自期三年归,
今已历九春。
飞鸟绕树翔,
嗷嗷鸣索群。
愿为南流景,
驰光见我君。

Poem

In the northwest lives a woman weaver,
who makes the most splendid silk.
At dawn you find her at the loom,
by afternoon, not a piece is finished.
Her sighs persist throughout the night,
her mourning cuts the blue clouds.
"I, a humble woman, retreat to the empty chamber,
while my lord goes abroad with the army.
Three years and I expected him back,
but nine springs are gone and I sit here waiting.
Birds are hovering round the trees,
chirruping for a mate.
I wish I were the southward-flowing sunshine,
riding, fast as light, to greet my lord."

门有万里客行

门有万里客,
问君何乡人。
褰裳起从之,
果得心所亲。
挽衣对我泣,
太息前自陈。
本是朔方士,
今为吴越民。
行行将复行,
去去适西秦。

There Stands a Visitor at My Door

There stands a visitor at my door.
"How far have you come?"
      "Ten thousand *li*."
I held my gown together, listening to his words,
for this was a man close to my heart.
He wiped away his tears with his sleeves,
and sobbed as he told his story.
"Originally I was a Northerner,
but today I am a subject of the South.
On and on, it's on and on we go,
and westwards, onwards, onwards,
      to the place of Qin ..."

闺情

揽衣出中闺,
逍遥步两楹。
闲房何寂寞,
绿草被阶庭。
空穴自生风,
百鸟翔南征。
春思安可忘,
忧戚与君并。
佳人在远道,
妾身单且茕。
欢会难再逢,
芝兰不重荣。
人皆弃旧爱,
君岂若平生?
寄松为女萝,
依水如浮萍。
赍身奉衿带,
朝夕不堕倾。
傥终顾盼恩,
永副我中情。

Feelings from a Boudoir

Gathering my robe I walk out of my boudoir,
and wander between the columns.
How lonely and quiet the spacious room!
Green grass covers the courtyard steps.
A draught blows through the silent room,
birds in their hundreds, heading south.
How can I forget the feelings of spring!
In anxiety and sorrow I am at your side.
My loved one travels a distant road,
and I, a humble woman, am left alone.
A happy reunion is hard to meet again,
the orchid's beauty doesn't bloom a second time.
People all desert their former love,
but will you be the same as in our old days?
The vine depends on the tree for life,
as duckweed does on the water.
I give myself to you to care for your belt,
so day and night it will not fall.
My heart would forever be satisfied
if only that loving glance of yours would endure!

情诗

微阴翳阳景,
清风飘我衣。
游鱼潜绿水,
翔鸟薄天飞。
眇眇客行士,
遥役不得归。
始出严霜结,
今来白露晞。
游子叹黍离,
处者歌式微。
慷慨对嘉宾,
凄怆内伤悲。

A Traveler's Song

The sun hides behind wisps of cloud,
my robes are lifted softly by the wind.
Fish swim in the clear stream,
and birds hang under the blue.
And I, bound by the corvée
can not go home, so far away.
When I left, the frost was hard,
and now the dew is quickly dried.
The traveler sings the "Lament":
    so desolate is this place.
And those who stayed, the "Song of Beseeching"[1]:
    begging him to return.
I am moved as I face these noble guests,
sadness spearing my innermost heart.

---

1 《黍离》、《式微》皆为《诗经》中的作品。"Lament" and "Song of Beseeching" are poems from the *Shi jing* or the *Book of Poetry*.

失题

双鹤俱遨游,
相失东海傍。
雄飞窜北朔,
雌惊赴南湘。
弃我交颈欢,
离别各异方。
不惜万里道,
但恐天网张。

A Poem

A pair of cranes roamed together,
by the Eastern Sea they were parted.
The cock escaped to the north,
in terror, the hen fled south.
Once our necks touched in love,
now we went to different lands.
It isn't the distance that daunts me,
so much as that heavenly net, spread wide,
      awaiting us.

译者简介

吴伏生，美国犹他大学中国文学及比较文学教授。著有专著 The Poetics of Decadence: Chinese Poetry of the Southern Dynasties and Late Tang Periods (1998), Written at Imperial Command: Panegyric Poetry in Early Medieval China (2008),《汉诗英译研究：理雅各、翟理斯、韦利、庞德》(2012),《英语世界的陶渊明研究》(2013),《迪伦·托马斯诗歌精译》(2014),《中西比较诗学要籍六讲》(2016), 并发表有关中国文学、比较文学的论文多篇。

格雷厄姆·哈蒂尔，英国诗人，曾在南开大学、卡迪夫大学、斯旺西大学以及伦敦 Metanoia 学院讲授英国诗歌及诗歌创作。著有诗集 Ruan Ji's Island and (Tu Fu) in the Cities (1992), Cennau's Bell (2005), A Winged Head (2007) 和 Chroma (2013), 并发表有关诗学和社保、医护与文学创作方面的论文多篇。

此书为吴伏生与格雷厄姆·哈蒂尔合作翻译的第三本著作。此前他们还出版过《阮籍诗选英译》(1988, 2006),《曹植诗歌英译》(2013)。

About the Translators

Wu Fusheng is professor of Chinese literature and Comparative Literary and Cultural Studies at the University of Utah. He is the author of *The Poetics of Decadence: Chinese Poetry of the Southern Dynasties and Late Tang Periods* (1998), *Written at Imperial Command: Panegyric Poetry in Early Medieval China* (2008), *A Study of English Translation of Chinese Poetry: James Legge, Herbert Giles, Arthur Waleyand Ezra Pound* (2012), *Tao Yuanming Studies in English-speaking World* (2013), *Selected Poems of Dylan Thomas* (2014), *Six Lectures on Key Works in East-West Comparative Poetics* (2016), as well as numerous articles on Chinese literature and comparative Literature.

Graham Hartill is an English poet. He has taught English poetry and creative writing at Nankai University, Cardiff University, Swansea University, and for the Metanoia Institute, London. He is the author of several poetry collections which include *Ruan Ji's Island and (Tu Fu) in the Cities* (1992), *Cennau's Bell* (2005), *A Winged Head* (2007), *Chroma* (2013), as well as many essays on poetics and creative writing in social and health care settings.

This is the third collaborative work of Wu Fusheng and Graham Hartill. Previously they have also published English translations of the poetry of Ruan Ji (1988, 2006) and Cao Zhi (2013).